Amy Cross is the author of more than 100 horror, paranormal, fantasy and thriller novels.

THE HAUNTING OF BRIARWYCH CHURCH

AMY CROSS

CONTENTS

THE
HAUNTING
OF
BRIARWYCH
CHURCH

PROLOGUE

"MAY THE LORD HEAR ME, and guide me through it all."

Keeping my head bowed, so as not to be noticed, I make my way along the corridor. Voices are shouting out in the distance, patients and nurses, as I head toward the exit. I can see the double-doors up ahead, and the glorious sunshine beyond, and now I am only a few meters away. If I just keep walking, and don't look back, I shall be fine.

"Father?"

Suddenly a hand touches my shoulder from behind, and I freeze.

"Father Loveford, where are you going?"

I half turn to look at her, but I already know that this is Nurse Simpkins.

"Father, why don't you come back this way

with me?"

"I -"

"Please, Father. You know it's important."

I hesitate, before turning fully and seeing her kind face smiling back at me.

"I know you weren't really going to leave," she continues, "were you?"

After staring at her for a moment, I turn and look once again along the corridor. The daylight seems so bright outside, and I can see the beautiful green gardens stretching out toward a distant treeline. And then, looking up at the panel above the door, I feel my heart sink as I see – etched in reverse in the glass – the name of this place:

Meadow's Downe Asylum

"Come on, Father," Nurse Simpkins says, moving her hand down to my elbow. "You don't need me to tell you, do you? You know you have to come with me."

CHAPTER ONE

One year earlier

FINALLY I SEE IT rising above the tree-tops in the distance, and my first reaction – instinctive, even, since it catches me by surprise – is to tap on the back of the driver's seat and call out:

"Stop the car! Please, stop right here!"

The driver dutifully pulls the taxi off at the side of the road. As the engine cuts out, I have to duck slightly to peer out through the front of the vehicle, but sure enough I can still see that tall, thin, beautiful spire silhouetted against a gray sky.

"I think I shall walk from here," I tell the driver, as I take my wallet from my pocket and remove two crisp, carefully-folded notes. "You may charge me as if we had gone all the way to

Briarwych, and by all means keep whatever change is due."

The driver grunts something that doesn't sound particularly grateful, but I do not care as I take my suitcase and clamber out of the taxi. Immediately, I am struck by the smell of countryside air, which is so very different compared to the London smog I left eighty miles away. Indeed, for the first time in many months, I can hear birds twittering in the trees, and I even take joy in the sound of my feet rustling in the long grass.

A moment later the taxi's engine starts up, and I wait as it turns around and drives back the way we just came. Then I am once again plunged into the calm and tranquility of the Kent countryside, and I take a few steps out into the middle of the road. There I stop and look at the beautiful church spire in the distance, and I take a deep, satisfied breath as I realize that after months of planning I have finally reached my destination.

Well, almost.

I am probably two miles from the village still, perhaps three at most, but I wish very much to approach my new home on foot. This is, after all, how the pilgrims would have arrived many hundreds of years ago, and in these dark and harried times I believe it is every man's duty to draw himself closer to those pious times. War might rage on the continent, but we cannot allow such horrors to change our way of life here in our dearest, most cherished England. And out here, right now, how could any man even imagine a place that is more perfect and peaceful?

With my suitcase in my right hand, then, I start limping along the road, heading toward the distant spire of Briarwych Church.

Toward the future.

CHAPTER TWO

"A NEW VICAR, EH?" the man asks, starting to walk with me along the steep curved path that leads up into the heart of Briarwych. "I don't think anyone round here was expecting a new vicar any time soon."

"Confirmation of my appointment came only last Thursday," I reply, as I feel a twinge of pain in my right leg. "I dare say my keenness to make the journey brought me here faster than the bishop could send a letter to the parish council."

"People'll be surprised," the man continues, "that's for sure. It's almost a year since Mr. Perkins went off to war, and since then we've been constantly promised that somebody would be sent down. I don't suppose you've heard anything about Mr. Perkins, have you? Last we heard, he was headed off to the front."

"I'm not sure," I reply evasively. The truth is, news came through just two weeks ago that Mr. David Perkins was killed in action near Ypres, but I do not wish my first act here in Briarwych to be the delivery of such awful news. I shall wait a while for that. "I can assure you that I am very keen to get started here in Briarwych. Very keen indeed."

Ahead, the spire looks much closer now, but the church itself is still hidden behind a row of gray-stoned houses.

"Is it your first church, might I ask?" the man continues.

"It is."

"I was thinking that. No offense intended, of course, but you do seem a little younger than the average."

"I hope I can make up for a lack of experience," I reply, wincing slightly as my right leg flickers with pain. "I humbly suggest that I am prepared for this position, and I do not think I would have been sent if anyone else had any concerns. Although I must admit, I had to fight a little to be assigned to Briarwych. There was some resistance to the idea of sending anybody here at all."

"Is that right?"

"Most likely because of the village's remote location."

"Aye, I'm sure that's it."

"To be honest," I continue, struggling a little to get any words out at all, "I rather wonder if the local RAF base didn't have something to do with it. This is the closest church and they themselves have been without a chaplain for some time now. Costs and all. So I'm afraid that to some extent I'll be pulling double-duty."

Reaching the top of the hill, I stop to regather my breath. That slope was somewhat more challenging than it appeared, and I must confess that I am perhaps not in the finest of health. An extended stay in hospital will do that to a man, no matter how hard he tries to recover in the aftermath. Indeed, as I lean for a moment against the wall, I can tell that my companion has already noticed my lack of fitness. He looks to be seventy if he's a day, but he – unlike me – is not out of breath after the climb.

"It's all hills round here," he says finally. "You'll get used to that."

He paused, before reaching out a hand.

"Roland Rose," he continues. "British forces, retired. Although I'd go back in a second, if they'd take me."

"Lionel Loveford," I reply, shaking his hand. "It's a great pleasure to meet you, Mr. Rose. I am so very much looking forward to serving the people of this fine community, and taking on the role of custodian of your fine church."

Looking along the street, I see that houses are still obscuring the view of the church, although the steeple remains tall and proud against a darkening sky.

"I have heard that this church is one of the finest in the whole of Kent," I continue, feeling a swell of pride in my chest. "Indeed, I am at a loss to understand why it has remained shut for these past few years. I would have thought that among the locals, there'd be a clamoring for somebody to come and open the place up again." I stare at the spire for a moment longer, before turning and seeing that Mr. Rose now appears a little apprehensive. "The church is the heart of a village," I add. "I've always believed that. I intend to get this heart beating again, for the sake of us all."

"Aye, I'm sure you'll do that," he says. "There'll be much to be doing, mind. I'm not sure how the place was left."

"I'm sure Mr. Perkins made the proper arrangements before he left," I reply. "A cleaner has been going in, has she not?"

"Not as far as I'm aware."

"Well, then..." I pause for a moment, before forcing a smile. "Whatever needs doing," I continue, "shall be done. That is the nature of our work for the Lord, is it not?"

"Aye, I'm sure," he says, and then he takes a

step back. "I won't detain you any longer, Mr. Loveford. I'll only wish you luck, and I'm sure I'll see you around soon."

"And at Sunday service, of course."

"Aye, and at Sunday service," he replies, with no obvious sense of excitement.

With that, he mumbles something under his breath and then walks away, heading up the hill and then disappearing along a side-street. He certainly seems to be a peculiar chap, but then I suppose we all do to some extent, when we meet strangers for the first time. I imagine this whole town will be a little wary of me at first, but I intend to win them over once they come to appreciate my stewardship of their fine church.

Now fully rested, I resume my walk toward the church. With each step, I feel a swell of contentment in my heart, as I realize that I am getting closer and closer to a house of the Lord.

And to my first parish.

CHAPTER THREE

OUTSIDE THE CHURCH, just before the gate, there stands an old noticeboard. Faded, yellowing notices have been left hanging behind the glass, so I stop and take a moment to slide these out. In truth, the noticeboard looks rather unkempt, and I'm surprised nobody had seen fit to tidy the place since Mr. Perkins left. Nevertheless, it is the work of a mere moment to pull the papers away, and already I am making improvements.

Looking down at the papers, I see that they contain announcements of various church events. I am rather surprised to see that they all date from around the end of 1940, which is a good year before Mr. Perkins left for military service. I am sure he must have organized events and services in the interim, but evidently for some reason he neglected to advertise these on the church noticeboard.

Never mind.

In the early days of war, much was likely overlooked.

After screwing the old pieces of paper up, I carry my suitcase through the gate and into the churchyard, where I find that the grass is overgrown. Indeed, the entire place looks completely neglected, with grass having been left to grow wildly around the gravestones. I am again surprised to see that – even in the absence of a local vicar – nobody from the village thought to come and maintain the church grounds in a proper manner, but I quickly remind myself that I should not judge too quickly. I am sure that the people of Briarwych have their reasons, and that they are good Christian people.

Nevertheless, I have to rather pick my way carefully between the gravestones as I struggle to find a path. Thick brambles have curled all across the yard, and I almost catch myself several times, but finally I spot the door at the front of the church and I reach into my pocket for the keys that I was given back in London. Evidently the church here in Briarwych has been left in a state of abandon, but I shall certainly get on top of this unforeseen turn of events. Indeed, as I get to the door I am already filled with a resolve to get immediately to work. Why, the day is still young and I can most certainly set to work in the afternoon.

Glancing down, I see several small pieces of masonry that appear to have fallen from the roof. Nobody has been to clear them up, and I suppose that I shall have to arrange for a full inspection to be made. After all, I cannot risk having any of my new congregation members being injured on their way to worship.

Just as I am about to turn back to the door, I spot movement in the window of a nearby house. I turn and look, just in time to see a figure stepping out of sight. A curtain falls back into place, but it is most certain that I was being watched. I look at several of the other houses, and sure enough another curtain moves similarly. I suppose that the fine people of Briarwych are simply besides themselves with excitement, now that the church is being reopened. Why, Mr. Rose has probably been hurrying around already, spreading the joyous news.

With that, I turn and slide the old iron key into the lock. I have to jiggle it around a little, and at first it will not turn. Just as I am beginning to worry, however, I feel the mechanism shift, and with a feeling of great honor and duty I push the wooden door open and – for the first time – I step into the magnificent Briarwych Church.

CHAPTER FOUR

THE FIRST THING I notice, as I enter the church, is that the air in here is very cold. I suppose the old stones walls provide no warmth whatsoever, and the church has been locked up for quite some considerable period of time. Still, the air is decidedly chilly, to the extent that I decide to leave the front door open in the hope that air from outside might enter and warm the place up a little.

But then I look straight ahead, and I see that this church is so much more beautiful than I ever could have imagined.

I have seen pictures of Briarwych Church, of course, but the reality is something else entirely. Setting my suitcase down, I simultaneously feel the weight of responsibility settling upon my shoulders. As I start to make my way along the aisle, I look up at the tall, beautiful stained-glass windows, and I am momentarily dazzled by the brilliant shades of red and blue and yellow that – even set against a dull gray sky – bring to life so wonderfully the stories that they are intended to depict.

Indeed, I am guilty for a moment of letting these wonders overwhelm me, and it takes a few seconds before I remind myself that there is more to a church than such wonders. Forcing myself to look away, I turn my attention instead to the wooden pews that are arranges on either side of the aisle, and I see old prayer books and kneeling pads that were evidently left scattered when the church was locked up more than a year ago. There are old candles, too, that were left melted on racks near one of the pews, and again I am surprised that Father Perkins did not see fit to tidy the place a little before he departed.

Then, again, I must remind myself to not judge people.

I make my way slowly along the aisle, keen to breathe in the calm, humble beauty of this church. After all, there is no need in this world to hurry, especially when one is all alone, so I take my time until finally I reach the foot of the altar and I look up to see a simple yet beautiful cross that must have been standing here this whole time, unobserved ever since Father Perkins last shut and locked the main door. For a few seconds, I am transfixed by the sight of the cross, and I am reminded of my lessons back in Oxford when I was first taught by Professor Hugo Clairthorne to see beauty in simple things.

How he would chastise me now, were he to see how I allowed myself to become distracted by the pageantry of the high windows.

"It's the simple cross that you must admire," he would tell me, as he told me so many times back then. "This is where your work for the Lord must begin, and it is where it will end also. Never forget that."

The cross before me now is made of stone, with ragged edge and a simple decoration of two lines that cross in the center. Evidently the maker of this cross felt no compunction to dress it up with elaborate designs, and for that I am thankful. This cross is welcoming me here into the church, and finally I get down and kneel, bowing my head and closing my eyes so as to show that I am the humble servant of this beautiful place. I remain in contemplative silence for a moment, while taking slow and measured breaths, and then I open my eyes and get to my feet. I make the sign of the cross against my chest, and then I turn and head back toward my suitcase.

I must get to work immediately.

***

My home here at Briarwych Church is to be this small room at the rear of the building. There is no rectory in the village, and I turned down the offer to be given rooms with a local family. I wish to be here on the church grounds as much as possible, to live and breathe my life here, and so I am more than happy to make do with this small, stone-walled room with just its single window overlooking the cemetery.

Taking another set of folded shirts from my suitcase, I carefully place the garments into the dresser drawer. There is something very calming and relaxing about performing such a simple task, and I am rather glad at this juncture that I do not have a housekeeper or some other type of woman to assist me with these matters.

It is good for a man to be self-sufficient.

Hearing a rustling sound at the window, I look over and see that ivy is trailing down and has begun to blow against the glass. I step over and examine the situation more closely, and I see that the ivy has indeed become very overgrown out there. Peering up toward the top of the window, I realize that I am going to have to acquire a ladder from somewhere, and that the task of improving the church's outward appearance is going to take a lot longer than a single afternoon. Somebody really should have been assigned to look after the place, but I suppose one must deal with matters as they are.

Just as I am about to return to my suitcase, however, I spot a series of scratches in the stonework at the base of the window.

Taking a closer look, I see that the stonework has been gouged away at the very edge of the glass, and some of the gouges have been stained with a dark brownish, slightly red substance. I reach out and run a fingertip against the marks, and I quickly find that they are rather shallow. Still, it is as if something was at one point clawing at the stonework in this spot, and I can only assume that the damage was caused by some over-vigorous cleaner. It is a shame to see such slovenly work, but I suppose that there is no reason to become agitated by matters that are in the past.

And then, as I stand at the window, a light rain begins to fall outside, tapping gently but insistently at the glass. After a moment, the rain becomes a little stronger, then stronger still, until finally there is a downpour. I suppose that some people might take this to be a bad omen, or might find the bad weather rather gloomy.

Not me.

No, I am already certain that Briarwych shall be conducive to peace, to good work and, above all, to a calm and ordered mind.

CHAPTER FIVE

SHELTERING UNDER THE TREE next to the gate, I take a moment to set the notice in place and then I swing the noticeboard's glass door shut. Despite the rain, and despite the generally disorganized appearance of the church, I felt it prudent to brave the bad weather and come out to post a note of my first service, so that the people of this fine village have time to anticipate the reopening of the church. Thus, I have kept the note simply and to the point:

*A warm welcome
is offered to parishioners
for a service with hymns
this Sunday the 18th
at 10 o'clock in the morning.*

Evening service at 6 o'clock.

Spots of rain are already falling on the glass, but I have no doubt whatsoever that by Sunday the weather will be bright and sunny. And even if it is not, I doubt very much that the people of this fine village will let anything keep them away.

"A service with hymns?" a voice says suddenly.

Startled, I turn and see that I have been joined by a rather scruffy-looking gentleman. With rain hitting the canopy of leaves above, it is no great surprise that he came up behind me without my having noticed.

"Lionel Loveford," I say with a smile, stepping toward him and reaching out to shake his head. "As you might have heard by now, I have been sent to reopen this fine church. I'm sure you'll agree that it was closed for far too long."

"Hmm," the man replies, shaking my hand but conspicuously not offering his name. Instead, he glances past me and looks toward the church's open front door. "Been in there already, have you?"

"I certainly have. And most beautiful it is in there, too."

"Find anything, did you?"

"Find anything?" I pause, rather stumped by the question, but then I suppose this man is merely making pleasant conversation. "The church is indeed very welcoming," I continue. "I have not as yet had a chance to admire the windows in detail, but I have taken a very close look at the altar and I must say that the cross in particular is absolutely magnificent."

"Hmm."

He continues to look past me, furrowing his brow slightly as he peers at the open door.

"I must confess, however," I add, "that there is some cleaning work to be done. I don't suppose that you know, do you, of a little lady who might offer such services in the village?"

"You want a cleaner?" Turning to me again, he takes a moment to clear his throat. "Looks to me like you're more in need of a gardener."

"I am not afraid of hard work," I advise him. "Do you know who used to clean the church, before it was shuttered? Perhaps the same person might be available again?"

"I highly doubt that," the man says, before turning as a young lady cycles past.

Blonde-haired and blue-eyed, the girl glances briefly at the man and then at me, but she keeps going on her way and quickly disappears around a bench in the road. I watch her go, and I must confess that for a moment I was rather struck by her striking, piercing eyes. She looked at me in a rather direct manner.

"I can do the grass for you, if you want," the

man says.

I turn back to him, having momentarily forgotten that he was here at all.

"I've got a good Atco Standard model that'll make light work of the place," he continues. "I could bring it round in the morning and get started, shouldn't take more than a day. I'll bring a lad to help, too." He looks toward the church once more. "I'd have done it these past months, but it'll be much easier now that the place has been opened up. And you really didn't find anything in there?"

"Find anything?"

"Well, you know..." He turns to me again. "The place was empty, was it?"

"There's some furniture," I tell him, "and a few old sheets, things like that. I rather get the impression that my predecessor left in a hurry."

"In a hurry?" He raises his eyebrows. "That's one way of putting it, I suppose. Obviously it's all fine in there now, though, so I suppose we don't need to worry so much. I mean, if..."

His voice trails off, and he stares for a moment longer at the church, as if he's lost in thought. Then, just as suddenly, he manages a smile and takes a step back, and then he slips his hands into his pockets.

"Best not be stuck out here in the rain for too long, eh?" he says. "I know my wife for one'll be furious with me if I get my best coat wet. I'll be around tomorrow with the mower, and I'm sure everything'll be just fine then, won't it? Looks like things are properly getting back to normal around here."

"I'm sure," I reply, watching as he walks away, although I cannot understand what might be worrying him in the first place. If I didn't know better, I'd almost think that he seemed fearful when he looked at the church, and nervous of getting too close.

Of course, that cannot be the case.

Briarwych Church is quite clearly such a beautiful, idyllic location, and no man in his right mind could possibly feel – when in the vicinity of the place – a shred of anything buy joy in his heart.

I double-check that the poster for the weekend's service is still in place, and then I head back toward the church. Rain is falling faster than ever now and the sky is darkening, and there is much that I still need to get done before tonight's black-out begins.

CHAPTER SIX

THUNDER RUMBLES HIGH ABOVE, but there is no lightning. As I sit at a desk in my makeshift room at the rear of the church, I glance out the window and see that sunset is well and truly upon us. I do not wish to cause trouble with the local ARP gentleman on my very first night in the village, so with a heavy heart I set my pen down and then I lean over to snuff out my solitary candle.

Immediately, the room is plunged into darkness.

In some parts of the country, churches are exempted from the blackout, but not here. With a top secret RAF base just a few miles away, Briarwych is regarded as a prime German target, so even here in the church we are required to have lights out at night. I was informed, before I came, that money might be found to permit blackout curtains to be put up, but I turned down that opportunity. I'm sure the money can be better spent elsewhere and, besides, I find the darkness to be rather pleasing and conducive to contemplation.

Then again, there *are* times with a torch might come in handy.

Looking down at my diary, I squint as I try to make out the words, but the task is hopeless. One must simply accept in these times that light is gone at night. Peering out the window, I see that rain is still crashing down, and at that moment I see lights being put out in a few nearby windows. Sure enough, the people of Briarwych are heeding the warning that we must all go dark. Certainly, nobody wants to risk aiding and abetting the German planes that even now are probably flying this way.

I get to my feet.

Thunder rumbles again.

Turning, I feel my way across this unfamiliar room. Away from the window, I can see nothing at all, although when I get to the doorway I look along the corridor and I am just about able to make out a faint patch of light at the far end, shining through one of the main windows near the door. I am rather grateful for that light, for it allows me to fumble along the corridor in the direction of the kitchen, from where I hope to fetch a glass of water. I should perhaps have taken more care earlier to learn the layout of these back rooms, since now in the darkness I am rather adrift.

Stopping suddenly, I listen to the sound of rain and wind outside, and then I turn and look back along the corridor as I realize I can hear a faint, persistent tapping sound coming from somewhere inside the church.

A leak.

Sighing, I begin to make my way toward the direction of the sound, into the darker and colder parts of the building. Here I am truly lost, and I have to run my hands against the icy stone walls in order to keep from walking straight into an obstruction. I can still hear the dripping sound in the distance, and I am certain that I am moving in the right direction. When I reach the end of the corridor, however, I have to stop for a moment and attempt to ascertain which way to go next.

The dripping sound is a little closer, but – as I turn around in the dark – I cannot quite determine the correct direction.

Thunder rumbles again.

A moment later, I hear a very faint humming sound in the distance. For a moment, I cannot imagine what this might be, but then I look up as I realize that the sound is passing overhead.

Bombers.

Perhaps ours, heading out to France.

Perhaps German planes, coming to bomb

targets in England.

I suppose there are those who can recognize the plans by the noise they make, but all I hear is a drone that is already receding into the distance. I wait, listening intently, until silence returns, and then – as a mark of respect – I remain standing completely still.

And then, quite suddenly, I feel something brush against me. Not something solid, exactly; more something made of air, something that rushes past in the darkness, heading in the opposite direction. The sensation is quite strange and most certainly abrupt, and can only be explained by a sudden draft of air.

I know I should simply go back to bed and investigate the water leak in the morning, but I worry that long-term damage could already have begun to take place. This church is old, and I fear for its structural integrity if water has been getting into the foundations. At the same time, I also know that I could end up spending the entire night wandering around in the dark without ever managing to find the leak, and that I would be better off getting some sleep and then looking for a wet patch in the morning. After all, the church has been empty for a couple of years now, and it is highly unlikely that this one storm will bring the roof crashing down.

With that in mind, then, I turn and start

feeling my way back toward the bedroom, even as rain crashes down outside with more force than ever.

CHAPTER SEVEN

MORNING SUNLIGHT CATCHES THE wet grass, but at least the rain has stopped as I start picking up chunks of fallen masonry from around the church's door. Night is barely over, but in these troubled times I am always up with the lark and relieved that the darkness is gone. Perhaps there is something childish in that sentiment, but I believe it is a feeling shared by many others. Those oppressive nights, when bombs could fall upon us from German plans at any moment, are never pleasant.

Suddenly hearing a creaking sound, I turn just in time to see that a young lady has entered the cemetery. I get to my feet, still cradling the pieces of masonry, and I am about to greet the lady when I realize that she is the same blonde-haired woman who cycled past yesterday.

"Good morning," she says politely, perhaps a little nervously, as she stops a few feet from me. "I'm sorry to bother you, but... I heard you might be looking for a cleaner."

***

"And here again," I explain to Lizzy, as I lead her into the kitchen area, "there seems to have been no work done for quite some time. So I'm afraid that the initial clean will have to be rather thorough. Somebody had even left a bicycle in here, so I don't think the place was really being used much as a kitchen back in the day."

I turn, only to see that she is still out in the corridor, as if she's reluctant to come too far into the building. She's looking around, and I can't help wondering whether she's been paying any attention at all.

"Is everything alright?" I continue.

She turns to me, startled.

"Oh, of course," she says, and now she hurries through and joins me. "Forgive me, I suppose I'm just surprised to be in here. I never thought..."

She hesitates.

"You never thought what?" I ask.

"Well, that I'd ever come in here again," she

continues. "After Father Perkins left, and considering the circumstances, I rather thought that perhaps the church would remain locked forever."

"It's a lovely old church from, I believe, the twelfth century," I reply. "The central part, at least. The north chapel came about a hundred years later, and the south chapel another hundred years after that. It's really a very striking example of a good old Norman church, and I think it'd be a terrible shame for it to be abandoned. Don't you agree?

"Absolutely, but..."

She hesitates again, before turning and looking out toward the corridor. Something is clearly on her mind, and I am about to ask what when, suddenly, she turns to me again.

"What was it like when you came inside yesterday?" she asks.

"What was it like?" I furrow my brow. "Well, it was cold, I must admit."

"But there was nobody here?"

"In the church?"

I wait, but now she is simply staring at me.

"No," I continue finally, "of course not. Why should there have been? The place has been empty and unused since Father Perkins departed."

"Well, yes," she replies, "that's what they say, but..."

Again I wait, and again she seems loathe to tell me exactly what is on her mind.

"You are not the first person to get that look on their face while talking to me," I say. "Is there something about Briarwych Church that I should know?"

She looks toward the corridor for a moment longer, and then she turns to me again.

"Was she really not here?" she asks.

"She?" I pause for a moment. "Who is *she*?"

She stares at me as if she can't quite believe my answer.

"There is only one key to this church," I continue, "and I can assure you that it is in my possession, and that it was given to me just a few days ago in London."

"Oh, I'm sure that's true," she replies. "It's just that we all know what Father Perkins did when he left here a couple of years ago. Everyone knows. I mean, he..." Again, she pauses. "He locked her inside."

"I beg your pardon?"

"That was two years ago," she continues. "Several people saw the moment when he left, when he pulled the door shut and turned the key, locking Miss Prendergast inside."

I cannot help but furrow my brow.

"Miss Prendergast," she says again. "That's when she was locked in."

"I'm terribly sorry," I reply, "but you're going to have to explain this to me. Who is this

Miss Prendergast woman, and why in the name of all that's holy would anybody lock her inside a church?"

"You really don't know?"

"Know what?"

"They sent you here without telling you?"

"Evidently this is the case," I say, trying to hide the fact that I am finding this all rather tedious. "I've never heard of a Miss Prendergast in my life."

She hesitates, before turning and taking a few steps away. She seems awkward, perhaps troubled, and it takes a moment before she turns back to me. There is, I think, a hint of fear in her eyes.

"She used to work for Father Perkins," she explains. "Nobody liked her. Oh, I probably shouldn't say that, but it's true. She was shrill and vicious. Even Father Perkins abhorred her, although he was far too well-mannered to say as much. In truth, I believe they're right when they say that by the end she was mad, quite out of her mind. I mean, I suppose that's why, in the end, when he locked her inside, nobody..."

I wait.

"Nobody what?" I ask.

"Nobody wanted to come and let her out," she continues. "Not at first. I was younger then, of course, but I heard people saying that she could stew in the church for a while. For a night, at least. I think at first it was seen as something of a joke. And then the next day, when she still hadn't found a way out, they said she could stay another night. And then it sort of went on like that for a while, until people started saying after a week that, well, of course she'd got out. That she couldn't possibly still be inside."

"Of course she couldn't," I point out. "If the woman was trapped, she would surely have called out for help."

"Nobody heard her call out."

"So she wasn't here, then. I'm sure she wasn't an idiot."

"The door remained locked."

"Then she got out some other way."

"There *is* no other way," she says, with a hint of desperation in her voice. "Oh, I know this all sounds dreadful, but after a time people just... Well, they just stopped talking about it."

I wait for her to explain.

"Excuse me?" I ask finally, supposing that I must have misunderstood. "They believed this woman to be trapped in here, and they just... lost interest?"

"I think perhaps they just assumed she'd found a way out," Lizzy says. "Nobody really wanted to get into it that much, so they stopped talking about it. Everyone sort of ignored the church, to be honest. Well, until..."

Again I wait, and again she says nothing.

"Until what?"

"Oh, it must have been a year ago," she says, with a hint of tears in her eyes. "I feel so bad whenever I think of it, but about a year ago some local children were playing in the cemetery. They'd been told not to, on account of pieces of stone falling from the roof sometimes, but you know what children are like." She takes a deep breath. "When they got home, they were scared and crying. Eventually they were persuaded to tell what had happened, and they said they'd seen..."

Her voice trails off.

"Do you know the window in the bedroom?" she adds.

"I do."

"The children were outside, playing. That window is very old and rather opaque, very hard to see through. It has lead passing through it, as you might have noticed. It's really not much of a window at all. But both children swore that they'd seen somebody standing there, as if watching them."

"Someone inside the church?"

She nods.

"But the church was locked," I point out.

She nods again.

"Well?" I ask. "Did somebody come inside and check?"

"Nobody had a key, and there wasn't much eagerness to break down the door. Besides, it had been almost a year since Father Perkins had left, so everybody knew that nobody could still be inside. But then, over the next few months, more people said they'd seen the same thing."

"A figure standing at that window?"

"Or sometimes at one of the other windows," she says. "There's one in the kitchen, too, and at least one other in the corridor. But each time, the same thing was seen. The vague outline of a figure, and just the slightest hint of a face."

"It must have been a reflection."

"I do not think so, Father Loveford."

"Then it was hysteria," I continue, "or perhaps foolishness. People can be inclined toward mischief from time to time, you know."

"Oh, I do know that, yes." She pauses. "I myself never saw this figure at one of the windows, although in truth I never really went out of my way to look. Like a lot of people, I preferred to keep my eyes averted whenever I had cause to pass along the lane the comes close to the cemetery. I suppose I was afraid."

"And when did these imagined sightings end?" I ask, unable to hide the fact that I feel a little irritated. "At what point did people tire themselves out and accept that nothing untoward was happening?"

I wait, but she simply stares at me.

"Out with it," I continue. "When did this all end?"

"The last supposed sighting of a figure at the window," she says cautiously, "was about... three days ago."

I feel a shiver pass through my chest.

"I think Mrs. Parfitt was walking along the lane and she glanced toward the church. She saw somebody at the window and, well, I believe I heard that she fainted due to the shock."

I let out a heavy sigh.

"Please," I say, "there's no -"

"It was this very window here," she adds, turning and looking at the window at the far end of the kitchen. "Three days ago, Miss Prendergast was seen standing at this very window, two years after she was last seen. Almost exactly where we're standing now."

CHAPTER EIGHT

"IF THE REMUNERATION IS sufficient," I say as I step out into the churchyard, "then I would be happy for you to start tomorrow." I turn to Lizzy, just as she comes out after me. "Is that acceptable?"

"You don't believe me," she replies, stopping at the start of the path. "I can see it in your eyes."

"I believe that *you* believe everything you just told me."

Hearing a creaking sound, I look across the cemetery and see that the gentleman from yesterday is arriving with his lawnmower, and with a young boy in tow. They're pushing the gate open and arguing as they struggle to get the mower through.

"However," I continue, turning back to Lizzy, "I should caution you now that I do not believe, in any shape or form, in the existence of ghosts."

"Because of your faith?"

"Because of common sense," I tell her. "I am a man of the cloth, and as such I have traveled a great deal throughout this country. I have stayed in homes that are hundreds of years old, in places where terrible things have happened, and I have never once witnessed any kind of spirit or apparition."

"That doesn't mean -"

"I slept here last night," I add, interrupting her rather rudely but unable to stop myself. "I slept in this very church, alone and in total darkness. I heard and saw nothing. There were no moans in the night, no clanging of chains, no doors slamming or floorboards creaking."

"That's not -"

"I did not at any point feel that I was being watched," I continue, determined to snuff out this nonsense at once, "and I did not see, out of the corner of my eye, any unexpected figures standing in the shadows. Nor did I hear ghostly whispers, or the rattling of chains, or any of the other nonsense that one tends to find in such stories. It was simply me, and me alone, and some drips from a leaky ceiling."

I wait for her to admit that I'm right, but she simply stares at me.

"Why," I add, "I believe that if a man – or a woman – were to truly meet a ghost, were to meet somebody who had died yet who now returned in spectral form... Well, I fear the only consequence would be madness. Yes, indeed, I believe anyone who truly saw a ghost would be driven mad by the vision."

"Perhaps you're right," she whispers.

"It seems Briarwych has suffered for lack of spiritual guidance," I point out. "Fortunately I am here now, and we can begin to get things back on track. Lizzy, I would be grateful indeed if you could spread the word about my upcoming sermon on Sunday. I think I know what theme I shall tackle, and I should like to think that most if not all of the village will be in attendance. That way, we can begin to knock this nonsense on the head."

"Scores of people have seen her at the window, and you call it nonsense."

"I do."

"And if -"

"And I shall not discuss it one moment longer," I add. "Now tell me, can I expect to see you here tomorrow to begin your new cleaning job? It's a simple enough question, but I would appreciate an answer. If you are unavailable for any reason, I am sure I can find somebody else."

Stepping back, she looks up at the church for a moment, as if filled with fear. She hesitates, and for a few seconds I feel certain that she will refuse to return.

"I shall be here tomorrow," she says finally.

"Are you sure? Can I rely on you?"

She nods. "Absolutely."

"Because you accept that these silly ghost stories are foolish nonsense?"

"Because I need the money," she replies. "And because I suppose that even if there were a ghost here once, the door has been opened now. Perhaps she is gone."

"There is certainly no dead body in the church," I remind her. "Surely that fact alone is enough to demonstrate that these foolish superstitions have no basis in reality?"

"I shall be here tomorrow," she says, before turning and heading toward the gate, passing the man and boy who are working on setting up the lawnmower.

Left alone in front of the door, I cannot help but feel exasperated by Lizzy's foolishness. She seems like such and intelligent and level-headed young woman, and I am truly shocked to learn that she entertains idiotic superstitions. Then again, perhaps this whole village has gone for too long without spiritual guidance, in which case I most certainly have some work to do. And as the lawnmower starts up, I head back inside and walk straight through to my desk, so that I can start again on the sermon I am planning for Sunday.

CHAPTER NINE

"SAFETY IN NUMBERS IS not safety from God's judgment," I whisper, as I read out loud from the sermon I have handwritten over these past few hours. "For judgment, when it comes, is judgment of how we have behaved, not of how we have managed to fit in with those around us."

I pause for a moment, digesting those words, and then I glance out the window.

The man with the lawnmower is still at work, and the young boy is dutifully running around after him and gathering the cuttings. I must admit that after seeing how decrepit the church looked when I arrived, I am relieved to find that some of the locals are finally helping out. I do not understand why they could not do the same before I arrived, but again I remind myself that later is better than never in these matters.

The young boy picked up another bundle of grass and then turned to run, but then he freezes as his gaze meets mine.

I smile and wave.

He stares at me with an expression of abject horror, and it takes a few seconds before his features soften. He looked rather relieved as he turns and hurries away, and I cannot help but roll my eyes as I look back down at Sunday's sermon.

"If your neighbor sins," I read from the page, "there is no change in your own duty to the Lord. If your -"

Suddenly I hear a loud bumping sound, coming from somewhere nearby. I instinctively turn and look over my shoulder, and it takes a few seconds before I realize that the sound seemed to come from somewhere inside the church itself, as if perhaps a door was hurriedly opened and the handle was allowed to bang against the wall. There should be nobody else here at the moment, of course, so I quickly tell myself that the noise was likely just something outside that sounded closer.

And then, as if to disprove that notion, I hear the same noise again, except this time it sounds closer and higher, as if it is coming from one of the rooms above the living quarters.

I hesitate, unwilling to give in to base superstitions, but then I get to my feet. Were I a lesser man I might fear the arrival of a ghost, of course, but I am hardly about to surrender to such stupidity. Instead, then, I head to the doorway and look out into the corridor, where I wait in case the sound returns. Already, I am beginning to have my suspicions about what might be afoot and – although I do not wish to leap to such a horrible conclusion – I cannot help but feel it is a coincidence that this strange noise arrives just a few hours after Lizzy was telling me that weak ghost story.

"Hello?" I call out. "Is anybody there?"

In my mind's eye, I am already imagining Lizzy hiding somewhere in one of the upstairs rooms, perhaps clamping a hand over her mouth in order to keep from laughing. She seemed like a nice girl, very sober and thoughtful, but all that chatter about ghosts suggests that she has another side to her character. Would it be beyond her to sneak back to the church and to try scaring me in this manner? I do not know her at all, really, so I cannot judge either way.

Cautiously, then, I step out into the corridor, and naturally my eyes are drawn to the narrow spiral staircase that winds up toward the upper floor and the bell-tower.

"Hello?" I say again. "If there's anybody there, I would appreciate a swift end to this tiresome game. I am working on a sermon."

After just a moment, I hear another bumping sound, and now I am more convinced than ever that somebody is upstairs. Sighing, but realizing that I am unlikely to be able to reason with some prankster, I head over to the door that leads into the stairwell and then I listen for a few seconds. I am tempted to simply shut the door and slide the bolt across, and to then wait for the miscreant to inevitably bang and call help since there is no other escape, but I am a man of the Lord and I would prefer to tackle the problem head on.

I start to make my way up the stairs, holding onto the rope that runs around the edge for support, and finally I get to the upper floor. There are several doorways leading off this corridor, while another set of steps leads up toward the bell-tower.

"Lizzy?" I call out. "Is it you? I hope you don't think that this foolishness can ever persuade me that ghosts are real."

I head to the first door and look into the room, but there is nothing there, not even furniture. There is certainly nowhere to hide, so I check the other rooms in order to satisfy myself that nobody is lurking. Then I head up the next set of steps until I reach the door to the main part of the bell-tower, where I find that the bolt is still in place and the padlock is still secure. I am the only person who can open this lock, and it is clear that nothing has been disturbed, so I am quite certain that nobody is up in the tower.

I pause, before heading back down into the corridor, where I take a moment to wait.

After several minutes have passed, I begin to realize that the miscreant must have already left. I thought I was being careful, but I suppose it's possible that somebody slipped away while I was checking the other rooms, in which case the joke is on me. I head over to the window and peer out, hoping to perhaps spot the perpetrator running away across the cemetery, but all I see is the man still working on the lawn and the child still collecting grass.

Sighing, I make my way up the last set of stairs, to the door that leads into the bell-tower. This door remains securely locked, and it's clear from the dirt and grime around the edges that it has not been opened in some time.

Heading back downstairs, I return to my desk and take a seat. For a moment, I consider grabbing the padlock key and going back up to double-check the bell-tower, but I know that nobody else could be up there so I remind myself that I mustn't be distracted. If somebody has been trying to fool me, they perhaps want me to waste time poking around, and I refuse to do that. I shall not be so easily tricked into believing superstitious nonsense. If somebody indeed wishes to make me look and act like an idiot, they are going to have to do a much better job.

Checking the clock on the wall, I realize that there is no point getting back to work on the sermon now. I rather think that it is time to dust of the bicycle I found in the kitchen, and to head out to introduce myself to my other parishioners.

CHAPTER TEN

"JERRY WOULD DO ANYTHING to get his hands on these designs!" Corporal Bolton shouts a couple of hours later, as he leads me across the airfield. Nearby, a fighter aircraft's engine is roaring. "Some of the stuff here is absolutely bloody top secret!"

"I'm sure!" I reply, struggling to keep from getting blown away as the plane's propellers whip up the air all around us.

"That's why there are extra blackout restrictions in place for Briarwych," Bolton continues, leading me toward a small building that – I hope – will offer us some shelter. "Can't risk Jerry spotting the airfield from above at night. Essential to the war effort, this stuff is. I mean, bloody hell, there are secrets here that nobody's allowed to know outside of the top brass. If you learned certain things about some of these plans, I'd bloody well have to shoot you!"

"How lovely," I mutter. "Nice to know that the war effort is going so well."

***

"We don't want a priest," Bolton says a few minutes later, as he hands me a cup of tea in the control room that overlooks the main runway. "Sorry to be blunt, old chap, but priests and chaplains and all that palaver... Well, they just get in the way, if you know what I mean."

"I..."

To be honest, I don't exactly know how to respond.

"It's not that we don't like priests at all," he adds. "It's more a case of finding them a little morbid."

"Oh."

"That's why we cut a bit of a deal with the chaps back at Bexley," he continues. "Rather than having a full-time chaplain stationed here, getting in our way and generally being a bloody nuisance, we agreed to have visits from the priest at Briarwych. Of course, then it turned out that there wasn't a priest there, which I suppose is where you come into the picture. Sorry about that. Still, chin up, eh?"

He raises his cup of tea and then takes a sip, before wincing.

"Hot," he adds with a grimace. "Mind yourself, Father. By the way, do you see that filing cabinet over there?"

I turn and spot a green cabinet next to the door.

"If you opened that and looked at any of the documents inside," he continues, "I'd have to shoot you."

I turn back to him.

"I suppose I shouldn't open it, then," I suggest.

"Smart man," he mutters. "Good. I like that."

"I should be very glad to come and serve this base in any way that you see fit," I tell the gentleman, whose tone and general manner I am beginning to find rather abrasive. "A regular service would be -"

"We don't need any of that."

"Perhaps a -"

"We're barely going to see you at all," he continues, interrupting me yet again. "There's the rub of it, Father. Some of the boys think it's bad luck to have a priest around. The last thing we want is for you to start blessing the planes or the missions, or anything like that. The only thing is..."

His voice trails off for a moment.

"Sometimes things don't go quite according to plan," he adds, "and that's when we might have need of some assistance. If somebody comes back injured, for example, or worse. Then we might need you at a spot of short notice, if you get what I mean."

"I believe I do," I reply.

"I'd like to say that it won't ever happen," he says, "but I know better than that. Like I told you when you arrived, the planes we fly out of here are quite new, sometimes even experimental. That's why Jerry'd like to bomb the place so badly, and it's also why sometimes things go wrong. I don't know how you are around people with burns, Father, but I should warn you that it's not a pretty sight. Often, I think it'd be better for the poor blighters if they just died instantly. I know that's what I'd prefer, but we don't get the choice, do we?"

"I suppose not," I murmur.

"So that's why I called you out here, really," he continues. "Just to, sort of, establish contact so that you're ready next time we need you. It seemed like the polite thing to do."

I nod. "Indeed."

"But let's hope we don't, eh? Let's hope the war's over by Christmas and we can all knock it off."

"That would be good news indeed," I reply.

"So how are you finding things out at

Briarwych, anyway?" he continues. "Locals aren't giving you any trouble, are they?"

"I have only been in the area for a few days," I point out. "I am starting to settle in, although these things take time."

"Of course they do," he says with a nod, before taking a sip of tea. "Seems like a nice little village, all things considered. One or two of the locals are rather bloody annoying, but that's probably true anywhere." He takes another sip, even though he clearly finds the tea to be still too hot. "All things considered, we're not -"

Before he can finish, there's a sudden roar nearby, and we both turn just in time to see a fighter plane flashing low above the building. Startled, I turn and look out the other window, and I watch – shaken, and not a little perturbed by the brief din – as the plane shoots off into the distance.

"Sorry about that, Father," Bolton says, clearly amused by my reaction. "The boys like to buzz us now and again. No harm, eh?"

I turn to him.

"You didn't notice anything unusual about that plane's underbelly, did you?" he asks, suddenly furrowing his brow.

"I confess that I did not," I reply.

"Jolly good," he mutters. "I'd have to have... Well, you get the idea."

"So you don't want me to lead a service?" I

ask, hoping to swiftly change the subject from the matter of whether or not I should be shot.

"Not really, Father. We don't like to think about things like that. Best just to get on with business. But like I said, there are times when we need a priest. I hope those times don't come soon, but I'm realistic." He takes another sip. "Sooner or later, something bad always happens. And that's when we *will* need you, Father. Have no doubt about that. Something bad'll happen soon enough."

***

"I hope you don't consider this to have been a wasted trip," Bolton continues, as I climb onto my bicycle ready for the gentle ride back to the village. "Better to get things straight, isn't it?"

"Indeed," I reply, while choosing not to tell him that, yes, I do consider this journey to have been something of a waste. "I'm sure you'll remember that I am always available to help, no matter the reason."

"I'm sure you've got your hands full in the village," he mutters. "Then again, you've got it easier than old Perkins, seeing as how you don't have to deal with that wretched Prendergast woman."

I turn my bicycle toward the road, but then I stop and glance over my shoulder.

"You knew her?" I ask.

"I met her a few times," he says, clearly not very impressed. "That woman loved coming out here to complain."

"About what?"

"What do you think? About my lads. She was convinced they were going into the village and causing trouble with the local girls."

"And were they?"

He shakes his head.

"Contrary to the stereotype," he says, "we actually have rules around here. And my lads are always too tired to go fraternizing with the locals. Now, if there were any Americans here, it'd be a different story. Randy buggers the lot of 'em, in my experience. But my lads know what's what." He shrugs. "Didn't stop old Prendergast coming out here and making accusations, though. If you ask me, she was the one who had sex on the brain, what with all the things she imagined my lads were doing. I can't say I was sorry when I heard she -"

He stops himself just in time.

"I don't reckon I'll finish that thought," he adds. "It wouldn't come out right."

"I'm sure she was merely a God-fearing woman who wanted to do the best for her community," I tell him.

He rolls his eyes.

Perhaps I should admonish him for this

cynicism, but I suppose it would not do to criticize a man who is so deeply caught up in our country's war efforts. Instead, then, I bid him a good afternoon, before starting the pleasant journey back to Briarwych. I must confess that my visit to the RAF base did not end as I had hoped, but at the same time I truly believe that those fine men are under stresses that cannot be understood by the rest of us. And when they need me, I shall be ready to offer them whatever assistance they might require.

For now, I have plenty of other work to do. As I cycle back to the village, my mind is filled with thoughts of what I might mention in my first sermon. And as I make my way through the winding roads that lead up toward the church, I cannot help but glance at the windows of the houses along the route. Now that night is falling, people are getting ready for the blackout. I stop at one of the corners and look through the window of the local public house, the rather oddly-named Hog and Bucket. People in there are finishing their last drinks and preparing to return home.

These are the children I must reach in my first sermon on Sunday. These are the ordinary, common people who need my guidance.

CHAPTER ELEVEN

OPENING MY EYES SUDDENLY, I stare up at the dark ceiling. I was asleep, but something stirred me, and a moment later I hear the loud banging sound again. Sitting up, I wait for a moment as the sound continues, and then slowly I understand that somebody is knocking on the church's door.

Climbing out of bed, I slip into my dressing gown and grab the keys, and then I head out into the corridor, barely managing to fumble my way along without slamming straight into the wall. As I reach the door, I take the keys and slide them into the lock, and then finally I open the door and find a breathless, panicking woman waiting outside in the darkness.

"Can you come?" she gasps, already reaching out and taking hold of my arm. "Please,

Father Loveford, it's my son! You must come at once!"

***

Elsewhere in the house a clock strikes one o'clock in the morning, as I sit next to Jack Neill's bed and watch a solitary candle burning on the nightstand. Blackout shields have been installed on the house's windows, but the Neill family still prefer to use as little light as possible, just in case they might inadvertently let some leak out and assist any passing German plans.

Next to me, young Jack Neill takes another slow, steady breath. He's only eight years old, but already he's confined to bed by a sickness that has left him pale and thin.

"I'm sorry my wife called you out," his father, Thomas Neill, says after a moment. He's sitting on the other side of the bed, watching his son's labored breaths. "There was really no need. Jack has these moments where his breathing gets difficult, but it always passes."

"There is no harm in calling for assistance," I reply, "nor in requesting the Lord's blessing."

"This is a fine way for us to meet," he continues. "When I heard we had a new man at the church, I intended to come over and introduce myself properly, but I didn't get the chance today.

And now here you are, dragged out of your bed at midnight, led here to sit with our son." He pauses for a few seconds. "Well, one of our sons. The other's older, he's off fighting."

He pauses for a moment, as if the thought of his other son has brought added sadness to his thoughts.

"Sometimes I think I see Anthony," he explains, "in the shadows late at night. Then I worry that this is some kind of omen, a sign that bad news is on the way. It hasn't been so far, though. I think my imagination is just over-active, that's all."

"That's entirely understandable," I tell him, hoping to soothe his concerns. "I'm sure the Lord will listen."

We sit in silence for a moment. I am already thinking that perhaps I shall be able to go back to the church soon, although I do not want to leave too hastily. Mr. Neill is an important figure in the village, and he will be a good ally as I work to return the local people to a path of godliness. If the stories about the church are anything to go by, superstition has been allowed to run absolutely rampant. It's hard to believe that some of the locals, driven out of their senses by a superstitious tale, have been actively ignoring the church.

"Might I ask you something?" I say finally. "Forgive me, but do you know of a lady who I believe used to live here in Briarwych? A lady by the name of Prendergast?"

Mr. Neill turns to me, and I can see from the look in his eyes that he knows exactly what I mean.

"You've heard about her, have you?" he replies. "I suppose that was inevitable. Who was it who told you ? Was it Mrs. Pease at the shop?"

"That doesn't matter," I say. "I intend to speak about fears and superstitions on Sunday, and I suppose it would help to know a little more about the woman who seems to have been at the center of some gossip around here lately."

"Judith Prendergast was a wretched woman," Mr. Neill replies, keeping his voice low as young Jack continues to sleep between us. "I should not say such things, but I do. Even her own family came to despise her, even Father Perkins. She took the words of the Lord and she twisted them for her own vicious purposes. You won't find many people here in Briarwych who are sorry she's gone, that's for certain."

"And where is she now?" I ask.

I watch his face carefully, searching for any hint of the truth as he remains silent. What I see – or at least, what I *think* I see – is a kind of sorrow and regret, perhaps even guilt.

"I have heard a story," I continue, "that Father Perkins locked her in the church when he left, and that -"

"Father Perkins was a good man."

"Of that, I have no doubt. Which is why I find it difficult to believe that he would have done such a thing."

"Judith Prendergast tormented him," Mr. Neill explains. "Nothing he did was good enough. When the sinners among us asked him for guidance, he would offer them kindness and hope, whereas she would insist that they were bound for Hell. For her, any sin was enough to condemn a man. Her reading of the Bible was unlike any other I have ever encountered, and she saw everyone around her as being wicked. Any time a parishioner went to confess a sin to Father Perkins, Miss Prendergast would go up to the bell-tower and ring the bells, to let the rest of the village know that our collective sin had increased. Why, one time she even..."

His voice trails off for a moment.

"One time," he continues finally, "she even suggested to Father Perkins that sinners should be killed, so as to cleanse the flock."

"That sounds rather extreme," I point out.

"When Father Perkins announced that he was going to war, she accused him of abandoning God. She told him that he would die out there in the war, and that she would run the church in his stead. That, I believe, is when he shut the door and left her in there, but it was out of frustration more than anything else."

"And then what happened to her?"

"I imagine she left when nobody was looking."

"There were other ways out, then?"

"I'm sure an intelligent, capable woman would have managed," he replies. "There are other stories in this parish, Father Loveford, but you should pay no heed to those."

"Some people say that she never left the church."

"And that is precisely the kind of story you must ignore. Of course she left. Why she then departed the village, I cannot imagine, but I suppose she is out there somewhere now, bothering the parishioners of some other place. Perhaps she felt ashamed by Father Perkins' rejection of her. There are those who say that their relationship was not strictly platonic, which would in her mind have been perhaps the greatest sin of all. Then again, one mustn't listen to gossip, Father, must one?"

"All men and all women," I reply, "seem these days to have a contradiction at the core of their character."

"Indeed it seems so," he says, nodding slowly. "I confess, I do not want to know where Judith Prendergast went after Father Perkins left for war. I am merely glad that she is gone." He pauses, before reaching over and stroking the side of his son's face. "Have you heard anything of Father Perkins, by the way? He was a dearly-loved man here in Briarwych, and we have all hoped for news of his safe return."

"I am not sure that I have any news to give," I reply, preferring to side-step the details of Mr. Perkins' demise for now. "I *am* sure, however, that my predecessor would have treated Miss Prendergast properly, even if her behavior became somewhat provocative. He would have risen above any personal feelings on the matter. I believe he was here in Briarwych for a little over two decades, was he not? He must have been greatly loved by the community."

"Indeed he was," Mr. Neill replies, "and -"

Before he can finish, Jack jerks awake and breaks into a coughing fit. I make to help him, but Mr. Neill waves me away, and I simply watch as he cradles his son tight.

A moment later, the bedroom door creaks open and Mrs. Neill steps into view, her face filled with concern.

"He's fine!" Mr. Neill splutters, but the coughs have seized the boy and after a moment I notice faint splatters of blood on the white bed-sheets. "He's fine! He's absolutely fine!"

CHAPTER TWELVE

"IT'S A DISEASE OF the lungs," Mrs. Neill says as she sets a cup of tea before me at the kitchen table. She is keeping her voice low, presumably so that her husband upstairs will not know that we are talking. "You will understand, of course, why we don't like people knowing."

"I shall mention Jack in my prayers," I reply.

"Thank you." She stops at the sink for a moment, and then she turns to me.

I wait, but her gaze drifts downward and after a few seconds I realize that she is looking at my right leg. This is not the first time I have had someone stare, of course, and I instantly know what is going through her mind. As a relatively young man in a time of war, I am accustomed to questions. Even to insinuations, sometimes.

"The nerves are badly damaged," I tell her. "A childhood deformity that has grown steadily worse over the years. I did try to enlist, but they would not take me. I tried in two other places as well, but alas it seems I cannot be used. When they learned of my vocation, all the officials told me that same thing, that I would be more useful staying in England and helping people through the horrors of war. But I did try to fight, I assure you."

"I believe you."

"There is always the chance," I add, "that they will grow more desperate for men, and that eventually even *I* shall be deemed acceptable."

"You sound as if you want to go to war."

"I want to serve my country."

"Are you not doing that now?"

"I suppose so," I reply, yet deep down I feel a niggle of doubt, as if some part of me feels that I am not doing enough. "People here at home still need hope, and I can give them that. There are -"

"Our other son is out there," she says suddenly, blurting the words out as if she has been holding them back.

Upstairs, Jack briefly coughs again.

"Our other son is out there at war," Mrs. Neill says again. "I should like to pray for him, of course, but sometimes I wonder what else I can do."

"The Lord listens. You must believe that."

"To all the prayers of all the mothers in all

the world?" she asks. "How can he possibly listen to them all at a time like this?"

"What is your other son's name?"

"Anthony." As she says the name, tears glisten in her eyes.

"If you would like," I continues, "we can pray together for Anthony's safe deliverance."

"I feel wicked whenever I do that."

"Why?"

"By praying for his safety, am I not merely condemning some other mother's son to death? After all, this is war. Soldiers must die. If Anthony lives, another must die. If Anthony dies, another might live. How can I pray for him, when I know that by so doing I might inadvertently send another soul to his death?" She pauses. "I can't do that. I haven't prayed for Anthony once, not since he went away. Does that make me a terrible mother?"

"Perhaps we should pray and -"

"I cannot."

"The Lord -"

"I have told you," she continues. "I cannot pray for Anthony, not if by so doing I harm another."

I open my mouth to tell her that she must not worry, but somehow I cannot get the words out. There is an answer to her dilemma, of that I am sure, but I cannot quite determine that answer. And when, a moment later, her son coughs once again upstairs, I feel a rather easy alternative come to mind.

"Perhaps for now we should pray for Jack," I suggest, "and for his suffering to ease a little."

She pauses.

"Yes," she says finally. "Yes, that I can countenance." She bows her head. "Please."

I too bow my head, although it takes me a moment to find the words. I rather feel that I have failed to offer proper comfort and guidance, but for now I shall do what I can.

"Lord," I say, keeping my voice low, "we ask for your mercy, for an innocent child rests in pain in this very house."

***

"Thank you for coming tonight," Mrs. Neill says a short while later, as I step out into the cold night air and then turn back to face her. She still has tears in her eyes. "Perhaps his coughs shall ease, at least for a while."

"I am sure the Lord heard our prayers."

"I do my best, just like everybody else, but if -"

Before she can finish, we both hear the sound of engines in the distance. We turn and look up toward the clear night sky, but there is no sign of any planes up there. They must be close, though, and for a moment I try in vain to distinguish the particular type of engines that we are hearing.

"Are they ours," Mrs. Neill asks cautiously, "or theirs?"

"I cannot say," I reply, still trying to determine where the planes are or, indeed, in which direction they are flying.

"Oh, the light!"

Suddenly she switches off the hallway light.

"I am sure nobody saw that," I tell her, turning and seeing her standing in the darkness.

"Better to be safe than sorry," she points out, as her son coughs once again upstairs. "We don't want to inadvertently guide them to the airbase, do we? I apologize once more for disturbing you tonight, Father Loveford. Thank you for coming."

"You know where I am," I reply. "Call on me any time, day or night. And please, sleep well, Mrs. Neill. I am sure the Lord has need of your work come morning."

With that, I turn to walk away, although at the last moment I glance back at her just as she begins to shut the door.

"Can I expect to see you at church on Sunday?" I ask.

"Of course," she replies, with a dutiful nod. "Good night."

She shuts the door, leaving me to stand for a moment on the garden path and listen as the distant engines begin to fade. I think perhaps they are heading in from the coast, which means that either they are our boys coming home from the mainland or they are Germans coming to bomb the cities. I remain completely still and silent for several minutes, as if somehow deep down I fear that I might attract attention if I make a noise, and then I listen as the engine hum quietens to nothing.

Dear Lord, can not this war end soon?

Turning, I walk along the path and out onto the quiet, dark street, and then I start making my way back up toward the church. Fortunately there is not far to go, and soon I am back in the cemetery, where the path is now clear and obvious as it winds its way between patches of freshly-mown grass. In the moonlight, gravestones stand out so brightly that I worry they might be seen from the air, although I suppose that is not likely. Still, as I approach the church and fish the key from my pocket, I cannot help but look out across the cemetery and wonder how it is that war can rage all around us, yet this pocket of England remains so calm?

And then suddenly I stop as I see a face at the window.

A chill settles in my chest. At first I tell myself that I am wrong, but with a growing sense of fear I realize that I am not wrong at all. As I stare at the window of the kitchen, around at the rear of the church, a patch of moonlight illuminates the glass and I can indeed see a figure standing on the other side, seemingly staring straight at me from inside the locked church.

"This is not possible," I whisper, trying to dismiss the image from my sight. "I am tired, I am imagining things."

Yet the figure persists, hazy through the old glass but most definitely there. So far, the figure has not moved, but the moonlight casts great shadows where the eyes and mouth should be. I know that room, I was in there just this evening, and I know that there is nothing near the window that could possibly resemble a human face or body.

Taking a deep breath, I tell myself that I must go closer, that I must prove to myself that this is some trick of the light. I refuse to be so easily scared, so I start making my way past the door and around to the far side of the church, and then I step off the path and tread across the grass until I am just a few feet from the window.

And still the figure is there.

In fact, I think the figure has perhaps turned its head slightly, so as to continue to watch me during my approach.

I swallow hard.

This cannot be.

"This is an illusion caused by the light," I whisper, although I can hear my voice trembling. It is cold tonight, but not so cold that I should shiver, yet I *do* shiver. And that can only be through fear.

I swallow again.

My throat is dry.

I force myself to take another step forward, and then another, until I am directly in front of the window. Now the figure, or whatever it is, stands only a couple of feet in front of me, albeit with the distorting glass between us. And whereas I had hoped to come closer and to see that there is no figure at all, if anything the impression is now *more* clear.

Still, I know that this cannot be real.

Steeling my resolve, I step even closer, until my nose is just inches from the glass.

I stare at the shadowy eyes, and in that moment I start to realize that perhaps they are not eyes at all, that perhaps they are merely reflections on a wall in the room. My sense of concern begins to dip just a little, yet I cannot entirely convince myself that what I am seeing is not a face. I tilt my head slightly, trying to get a better view, yet still those two apparent eyes are staring at me.

Finally, I step back.

No.

No, this is not a face. There is nobody on the other side of this window. Of that I am certain.

I turn to walk away, but at the last moment I spot movement in the corner of my eyes.

I turn back.

Suddenly the face distorts and shrieks, rushing at the window. A scream rings out, and I step back with such alacrity that I trip on the edge of a gravestone and fall, clattering to the ground and landing hard on the grass. And as I stare up at the window, I see that the face is now entirely gone.

***

"Who's there?" I call out angrily as I push the door open and step into the darkened church. "I demand to know who you are and what you're doing here!"

Stopping, I listen out for any hint of a reply. It is now clear that some local prankster sees fit to toy with me, and I refuse to tolerate such childish behavior. Breathless and unable to contain my fury, I take a step forward and wait for the miscreant to repent, but all I hear is silence. The inside of the church is so very cold, but after a moment I turn and swing the door shut, shutting out what little light there was and plunging myself into darkness.

I instinctively reach for the light-switch, before remembering at the last moment that I cannot turn on any lights at all. Not during blackout hours.

Turning, I look ahead.

The stained-glass windows do not permit much moonlight to enter the church, so I am almost entirely left in darkness as I take a first cautious step toward the rearmost pews. There I stop, and as my eyesight adjusts to the lack of light I am just about able to see the various rows spreading out ahead toward the altar. I see no sign of anybody and, although it is possible that the trickster is hiding cleverly, I turn after a moment and look toward the corridor that leads toward my living quarters.

Heading back to the door, I slip the key into the lock and turn it firmly, and then I remove the key again. Whoever is in here with me, they shall most certainly not be able to run away without facing up to the consequences of their actions.

Stepping toward the corridor, I make my way to the kitchen and look through, and I immediately spot the window at which – just a few minutes ago – somebody stood in this very room and watched my approach. Now, however, there is no sign of anybody, although I am certain that the person cannot have gone far.

I walk to the window and look out for a moment. The glass is so old, it is impossible to get a proper view, but I can just about make out the shapes of the nearest gravestones. Somebody standing here would certainly have been able to see me, and would doubtless have made out the astonished look on my face as I fell. I suppose that was the intended reaction, in which case I am sure that the perpetrator of this hoax would have enjoyed a hearty chuckle.

Now, however, the fun and games are most

certainly over.

Suddenly hearing a brushing sound, I turn and look over my shoulder. There is no sign of anybody, and the sound of has passed, but for a moment I am sure that I heard a faint ruffling noise, as if perhaps someone walked along the corridor and brushed briefly against one of the stone walls.

I head to the door and look out, checking both directions, but there is of course still no sign of anyone.

I wait, listening in silence for the intruder's inevitable next mistake.

"Do you think I am a fool?" I call out finally, even though I know I should probably stay quiet. I am simply too angry to hold back, and as I step out into the corridor I cannot help thinking of somebody hiding nearby and trying to stifle a giggle. "This is a house of the Lord, and you think it is your right to play games? Shame on you. I demand that you come out and explain yourself, and then – if you are willing – I might be persuaded to help you repent!"

I wait.

Silence.

"You are testing my patience!" I announce. "Let me assure you, any pleas for forgiveness will seem more genuine if they are made after you reveal yourself, rather than if they come after I have rooted you out from your miserable hiding place.

Do you think the shadows will protect you for the whole of the night?"

Again I wait.

Again, there is no reply.

"If not -"

Suddenly I hear another bump, and as I turn I immediately realize that the sound has this time come from somewhere above. I spot the open door that leads to the stairs, and in that moment it becomes more than apparent that the miscreant has fled to the upper floor.

"You think you're safe up there, do you?" I mutter, before starting to make my way over. "We shall see about that."

I begin to climb the stairs, but then I stop myself. I hesitate, and then I step back. I could go up, of course, and search the rooms one by one. In this darkness, however, I could easily lose sight of the intruder, who might indeed double back and slip away. Indeed, if there is another way out of the church, the intruder might be able to escape without being seen, in which case I would seem like quite the fool. Whereas if I watch the stairs, I know for a fact that the intruder cannot pass undetected back down to the ground level, in which case he or she shall be quite trapped and shall have no choice but to eventually confess.

Therefore, I step back from the stairs and resolve to remain here all night if necessary. Sooner or later, the miscreant has to make their move.

Heading to the door, I take the wooden chair from next to the alms table and I sit so that I can see the foot of the stairs. There is now no escape for the intruder. Even in darkness, I shall be able to spot any man or woman who tries to get away. And if the intruder believes that I shall move even one inch from this spot until then, they shall swiftly find that they have another thing coming.

AMY CROSS

CHAPTER THIRTEEN

THE BANG ON THE door behind me is sudden; so sudden, in fact, that I am startled as I continue to stare at the foot of the stairs. Morning light is streaming through the windows, and thus far – after several hours in this position – I am positive that the intruder has not come down from the upper level. And I most certainly did not fall asleep.

Did I?

Not even for a second?

No, I'm sure I didn't. I'm sure I kept my eyes wide open the whole time.

A moment later there is another knock, and I realize I can hear somebody shuffling about outside the door.

Getting to my feet, I move the chair out of the way and then I unlock the door. I do not know who can be here at this early hour, since it is not yet even seven o'clock, but when I pull the door open I am presented with a rather welcome face.

"Lizzy," I say, momentarily stunned. "I..."

"Am I too early?" she asks, taking a step back. "I'm sorry, perhaps I was too eager to get started with the cleaning work. You did say to come as soon as I was ready, but I can return a little later if you wish."

"Cleaning?" I hesitate, and then I realize that I did indeed make arrangements for her to come today. "Of course," I stammer, stepping back and pulling the door fully open, allowing her to come inside. "You must forgive me, I was rather lost in thought."

I look again at the stairs, where there is still no sign of the intruder having come down. In an instant, the whole situation feels utterly ridiculous, yet at the same time I know that I did not fall asleep during my long wait.

"Father Loveford?"

I turn to Lizzy, but how can I explain all of this to her? How can I tell her that I allowed myself to be spooked in the night? After all, that is what happened, and the last thing I want is for the people of Briarwych to start gossiping about how their new priest is already spreading fresh fear of a ghost in the church.

"Might I ask you a favor?" I say, as I start to

formulate a plan that should take no more than a few minutes to implement. "Would you mind waiting here for just a moment?"

***

"Well?" she asks as I come back down from the upper floor. "Did you find whatever you were looking for?"

"No, I did not," I reply, as I stop and try to work out whether there is any other way that the intruder could have escaped.

I checked every room up there, and I know that there is no way out through any of the upper windows. I did not try the bell-tower, but I have the only key to that padlock and I can tell from the dust and dirt all over that door that nobody has passed that way in quite some time. In which case, I am at a loss to understand how last night's intruder could possibly have escaped.

One thing is certain, however.

I do not believe in ghosts.

"There is no other way out of here, is there?" I ask.

"No, Father, there is not." She pauses, keeping her gaze fixed on me. "Why? Has something happened?"

"Is there no window, perhaps, that could be opened to allow one to slither out?"

She shakes her head.

"So the only way in and out is through that door?" I add, pointing toward the large wooden door at the far end of the corridor.

"Yes, Father."

"Then..."

My voice trails off. I know that I was awake all night, and that nobody could have slipped past me. Equally, I know that there is nobody else here now. I might have been rather exhausted of late, but it is hard to believe that I could have imagined that face at the window, or that my subconscious mind could have somehow summoned up that terrible scream that I heard.

Yet as I turn and look once more at Lizzy, I realize that any further questions are bound to rouse her suspicions even further. I want to end this superstitious nonsense, not add to it.

"Father -"

"Never mind."

"But if -"

"Everything is fine," I say firmly. "What did you say you wanted, again?"

"To clean, Father," she replies, rather matter-of-factly. "Today's my first day."

"Of course. I'm sorry, I was momentarily distracted."

"So can I get started now?" Lizzy asks, clearly bemused by my behavior. "I don't mean to push, it's just... I was planning to really give the place a proper going over, seeing as how it's been so long since it was cleaned. I brought some supplies, and I'm not afraid of hard work."

"That's fine," I reply, still half-thinking about the events of the past night. "I must work on my sermon for tomorrow's service, anyway."

"I shall try not to disturb you."

"Work as you must," I say, heading through to the office area. "Thank you, Lizzy. I greatly appreciate your devotion to this task."

Once I am in the office, and once I have heard Lizzy going through to the store-room, I stop at the desk and try once more to make sense of the sounds I heard last night. Unless I am losing my mind, it seems clear that somebody – somehow – managed to slip past me. I know of no other way in or out of this church, yet that is the only possible explanation. I feel I am at the verge of losing my wits, but at the same time I am quite determined that I shall not let this annoyance become a long-standing irritation.

I have a sermon to write.

Yet, as I prepare to put pen to paper, I suddenly become aware of voices outside the window.

CHAPTER FOURTEEN

"JUST PUSH HARDER!" the gardener says, his voice spilling over with irritation as he pushes the lawnmower across the overgrown cemetery. "Like that, see? Put some welly into it!"

Stepping back, he lets the boy take over, and he folds his arms across his chest as he watches the resultant efforts. He barks some more orders at the boy, and then he rolls his eyes as he turns and comes over to join me outside the church's main door.

"Apologies, Father," he mutters. "We didn't get it all done yesterday, on account of that lad being bone-bleedin' idle."

"No apology is necessary," I reply. "It's good to see a boy doing some hard work."

"He's a moaner, though, Father. You watch,

109

soon enough he'll be complaining about how his arms are aching and his legs are tired and how he just can't keep going. I'm telling you, children these days are losing the appetite for honest hard work. I don't know what the next generation'll be like if there's not an improvement."

"Indeed."

"Then again, the grass *is* long," he adds. "I suppose one of us should've come in and neatened the place up now and again."

"I understand that a local superstition was responsible for people staying away," I reply.

He eyes me with caution for a moment.

"Heard about that, did you?" he mutters finally.

I can't help but smile.

"Bits and pieces," I admit, as I watch the boy struggling still with the lawnmower. He makes for a rather comical sight as he huffs and puffs his way around to the other side of the church, disappearing swiftly from view. "I take it that some of the more over-excitable members of the local community have taken to spreading tales."

I chuckle as I turn to the gardener, but then I see that he's staring back at me with a stern expression.

"What is it?" I ask, still smiling. "You don't believe the stories, do you?"

"I saw her," he replies.

"I beg your pardon?"

He pauses, before stepping back and looking at one of the nearby windows.

"I saw her," he says again, his voice heavy with tension as he keeps his eyes fixed on the window. After a moment, he points. "Right there, about nine months ago."

"And you're sure this was not a reflection?" I ask.

"It was no reflection," he replies, turning to me again. "I remember Judith Prendergast. I saw her around often enough, even though I didn't really like to. She was a tall, thin woman, very proper. Good posture, looked like she was always carrying a bunch of invisible books around, balanced on the top of her head." He pauses, as if the memory is unsettling him. "So when I saw her at that window, a little over a year after she'd been locked inside, I recognized her straight-away."

"But if -"

"There's no doubting it, Father," he adds. "It was her alright. As God is my witness, I was not drunk and it was not dark. It was daylight, in fact, much like right now, and she was right there in that window. The question is, *how* was she there. She couldn't have used the main door, and that's the only way in and out of the church. And she certainly couldn't have lasted inside for all that time. Now, I'm not a man who believes in a load of nonsense usually, but I'll admit between the two of us that I felt mighty uneasy that day."

"So you're suggesting that Miss Prendergast spent two years inside the church?" I reply. "Just... watching?"

"Not *just* watching, if you ask me. Waiting."

"Waiting? For what?"

"That's what I don't like to think about. She was a nasty woman, and she made poor Perkins' life a misery."

"I was under the impression that he employed her as a general housekeeper and cleaner?" I reply.

"He was probably too scared to give her the heave-ho," he mutters. "That woman thought she should be in charge of every aspect of life in the village, she stuck her nose into everything and that kind of behavior really sticks in your craw after a while, doesn't it? She wasn't afraid to give her opinion on everything everyone was doing. You couldn't wear a pair of odd socks without her telling you God was watching and that you'd be damned to Hell. If you ask me, that woman had no soul."

"Everyone has a soul," I point out.

"Not a good one."

"It is not for us to judge our fellow man," I tell him. "We must remain charitable at all times, and conscious that others might suffer in private."

"Good riddance to the woman, if you ask

me," he replies, before turning as the young boy emerges from the other side of the church, having finally managed to push the lawnmower all the way around the building. "No-one misses her, and no-one particularly wants to know what happened to her. Just so long as she doesn't come back any time soon, we're all happy."

"One hopes that she is safe, at least," I point out.

"One should," he mutters, "but one doesn't."

"You can't possibly mean that you -"

"Get a move on!" he yells, waving at the boy. "Put some welly into it, or you'll never get finished! Flamin' Nora, you couldn't be slower if you tried! You'll be on a hiding to nothing if you want getting paid after this dismal performance, let me tell you. Let me show you how to handle the damn thing properly."

With that, he sets to work with the lawnmower, pushing the boy aside and then demonstrating to him how best to use the machine. I watch for a moment, and – although I can certainly appreciate the man's strength – I cannot help but think back to the quite heartless things that he said about this Judith Prendergast woman. It's almost as if hopes she is dead, which would be a most un-Christian way to view the matter.

I can only hope that his view is an outlier, and that he does not represent the opinion of the whole village. Could one woman really have been so awful that people wished her dead?

CHAPTER FIFTEEN

"FATHER LOVEFORD?"

Looking up from my journal, in which I have been writing out the sermon's latest iteration, I see Lizzy standing in the doorway. She looks rather unkempt, with her hair tied back and sweat on her brow, and with her sleeves rolled up and wet patches on her dress. Evidently she has been working hard over the past few hours, which I note is a sign of very good character.

"I'm so sorry to disturb you," she continues, "but I was cleaning in one of the upstairs room, and I couldn't help but notice something that I think you should see."

"What is it?" I ask.

"I... I would rather show you."

"Can you not simply tell me?" I ask. "I am

in the middle of some important work and I was rather getting into the flow."

I wait, but she looks rather uncomfortable.

"As you please," I say, getting to my feet and heading over to follow her. Evidently she is distressed by something, and it might be quicker to simply indulge her. "I have been up there a few times myself, and I must say that I have noticed nothing out of the ordinary."

She mumbles something under her breath, but she is already leading me toward the stairs and I can tell that she is troubled. Even though I barely know the young woman, I *do* know when somebody is upset. When we reach the top of the stairs and she gestures for me to follow her into one of the smaller rooms, I rather fancy that she appears very pale. Perhaps her constitution is weak.

"What's wrong?" I ask. "Did you perhaps come across a spider? They won't hurt you, you know."

"There," she says, pointing up toward the top of the wall. "Do you see it?"

Looking up, I see only the white plaster and what looks like a dark brown stain. I look around the stain, in case there is a spider or some other creepy-crawly that might terrify a young woman, but then I realize that the stain itself must be the object of Lizzy's discomfort.

"This is an old building," I explain. "There

is bound to be some discoloration."

"But it looks so different to anything else, and it seems to be coming from above."

"There is only the bell-tower above," I point out, "and I have not been up there yet. I doubt that anything is leaking down."

"I saw a mark like this once before," she says. "That is why I recognized it immediately. It was at a hospital where some blood had been spilled and not cleaned up."

"Blood," I remind her, "is red, not brown."

"But over time it changes color, Father Loveford. That's what I'm saying. The stain looks like *old* blood."

"And why would it be up there on the wall?" I ask.

"I fear it might be on the floor of the room above this one."

I open my mouth to calm her fears, but deep down I am starting to wonder whether she might be right. Truthfully, I did not notice the stain earlier, and I cannot now dismiss it out of hand. Indeed, I am already reaching into my pocket, already taking out the key that I shall need in order to open the padlock.

I do not wish to indulge Lizzy's fears, but it might be as well to show her that she is wrong.

"Wait here for one moment, please," I tell her, as I head back out and start making my way up the next set of steps, toward the old door that leads into the bell-tower. Truth be told, the climb is rather awkward, since the ceiling is low and the walls move noticeably closer. I suppose these old buildings were rather bodged together.

As I get to the door and start opening the padlock, I hear Lizzy coming up behind me.

"There really is nothing to worry about," I continue, struggling for a moment with the key. The padlock is old and slightly rusted, and clearly has not been touched for quite some time. "I intend to put your mind at rest, Lizzy, and then you must get back to work. One can find endless distractions if one is so inclined."

I turn to her.

She stares up at me with fear in her eyes.

"There is nothing up here," I tell her, forcing a smile in an attempt to calm her worries. "I promise."

I wait, but she is clearly not in the right state of mind to be persuaded. She must be *shown* that she is wrong.

Sighing, I fiddle with the key for a while longer, but then – just as I am beginning to fear that the lock is beyond use – I hear a clicking noise and the padlock opens.

Pulling the door open, I am confronted with another, smaller set of steps, leading up into the bell-tower itself. I should have come up here already, but I suppose I was trying to focus on important immediate tasks, while delaying everything else.

I gesture for Lizzy to wait behind, and then I begin to climb up, struggling slightly with the creaking wooden steps. The stairwell narrows considerably, to the point that I have to really hunch down in order to progress, and this is not made any easier by the fact that one of my legs is rather stiff. Finally I haul myself up into the cold, airy bell-tower and I look up to see that the bells all look to be in good working order. Filled with a sense of relief, I examine the ropes for a moment and then I turn to look at the spot directly above the stain in one of the lower rooms.

And at that moment I freeze, as I see a strange shape on the floor. It takes a moment, and then I realize that this shape is that of a curled human figure.

"Father Loveford?" Lizzy calls out. "Are you okay up there?"

I stare at the body, unable quite to process what I am seeing, until suddenly I hear Lizzy on the steps.

"Wait down there!" I shout.

"Is everything alright?"

"Wait down there," I say again, as I take a couple of steps toward the body. "Whatever you do, do not come up here."

"Why?"

"Just do as I tell you," I say firmly, stepping closer still to the body until I can make out the side of its face. "For the love of God," I add, "do not come up."

Wearing a ragged and pale gray dress, the body is almost completely rotten. Or perhaps that is not the right word. I am no expert, but the body looks terribly withered. I can see one side of the face, where the skin clings to the skull. The eyes are open, although I see no eyeballs, and the mouth is open too, allowing me to spot a row of stained teeth. Long dark hair is still attached to the scalp, and runs down to cover the neck and part of the shoulder. A little further down, the left hand is closed almost into a fist, with the fingers partially curled.

A breeze blows through the arches and through the bell-tower, and for a moment I detect a faint odor. At the same time, the fabric of the corpse's dress is rustled slightly, and some of the hair moves in the wind.

Crouching down, I see that the wooden floor beneath the body is stained a dark color. There is definitely blood, mostly around the head area, as if perhaps there is an injury unseen on the side of the head that is pressed against the floor.

Taking a deep breath, I make the sign of the cross against my chest, and then I lower my head.

"Lord, grant peace to this poor child of

yours," I whisper, "and take her into our kingdom. And have mercy on those who -"

"Is everything alright?" Lizzy calls out, and suddenly I once again hear her coming up the steps. "Father Loveford?"

"Wait!" I gasp, turning to stop her. "Don't -"

But I am too late.

She appears at the top of the steps, and her gaze immediately falls upon the corpse. She stares for a moment, her smile half-frozen on her face before fading entirely.

And then the poor girl screams.

CHAPTER SIXTEEN

"WELL, IT'S A WOMAN," Doctor Sommersby says as two attendants carry the covered body outside on a stretcher. "I'll have to make a formal identification, of course, but the age and height and general appearance, from what I can tell, match Judith Prendergast perfectly. The dress also matches the one she was last seen wearing."

I watch as the stretcher is carried out of view. A sheet covers the body, but I cannot help thinking of the terrible sight that I witnessed up there in the bell-tower.

"How long?" I whisper, before turning to Doctor Sommersby.

"How long has she been dead?" He pauses. "Two years seems about right. The conditions up there were very dry, and she was high enough up that any odor would have dissipated without being noticed by anyone on the ground. There would have been flies and maggots, that sort of thing, but again they were all the way up there in the bell-tower. It's not hard to understand how she could have died and rotted up there without being noticed."

He pauses again.

"Then again," he adds, "the condition of the body *is* a little different to what you'd expect. There'll be some reason, something in the environment up there, but I would have expected more... Well, I won't go into the details, but let's just say that she has more meat on her bones that I'd have thought."

A shudder passes through my chest.

"There's a wound on her head," he adds.

"I thought as much," I reply.

"It's right here," he says, tapping the left side of his forehead. "There's some blood on the corner of the ledge near the steps, too. I don't want to rush to judgment, but I wouldn't be surprised if she fell and hit her head on the corner. It's unlucky but not impossible, and she could have died instantly."

"But the padlock," I reply. "How could she have locked the door after herself?"

"The door itself was locked, yes," he says, "but the actual frame was loose. Didn't you notice? It can be pulled aside, certainly far enough to let someone get through even if they didn't have the key. Why she put it back in place after herself, I have no idea, but that's for the police to think about. People do strange things sometimes, Father Loveford, as I'm sure you're aware. We don't know why she went up to the bell-tower either, do we? Then again, she was rather fond of ringing that thing, whenever she wanted to draw attention to more sins in the village. Maybe that's why she loosened the door. If Perkins tried to lock her out of the tower, she'd have wanted to find another way in."

"I suppose so," I reply. "It's still hard to believe that the poor woman could have been up there for two years, undisturbed and undiscovered. Was nobody looking for her?"

"It's sad, to be sure." He nods, and then he sighs. "Clark's outside, I expect he'll want to have a word with you, but I don't think the police are going to be too interested in this case. It's open-and-shut, as far as I can see. Unless I find anything else during the autopsy, I imagine I'll have to list misadventure as the cause of death. It's a damn shame. The woman was disliked by pretty much everyone, but still, nobody should have to die like this. Makes you wonder, eh?"

With that, he turns and heads outside, and a moment later I hear him conversing with Constable Clark. Their conversation sounds unhurried, and it's clear that Miss Prendergast's death is indeed being treated as a tragic accident. I turn and head away from the door, and then I stop as I realize I can hear a faint, gentle sobbing sound coming from my office.

I walk to the door, and I see that poor Lizzy is indeed weeping with her face in her hands. She is sitting in my chair, in the spot where I have been sitting while I work on my sermon.

"There," I say, making my way over and, after a moment's hesitation, placing a hand on her shaking shoulder. "One must keep a stiff upper lip in these circumstances, mustn't one? I know it was quite a shock, but no good can come of this excess of emotion."

She looks up at me, and I see tears streaming from her eyes and running down her reddened face. In that moment, I feel that my words – particularly my warning about an 'excess of emotion' – sounded rather uncaring, perhaps even old-fashioned.

"No good?" she asks breathlessly. "Did you see her up there?"

I nod.

"Did you see her face?"

Again, I nod.

"Did you see how shriveled she looked? Her mouth was open and -"

"Well, there's no point going into detail," I point out, hoping to bring her to her senses. Were she a man, I would offer her a small shot of whiskey, but I don't think that would be appropriate in these circumstances. Instead, I leave my hand on her shoulder for a moment longer, for longer than I would in any other situation, and then I step back a little. "Nor is there any point in reliving the sight over and over."

I wait, but still Lizzy sobs.

"Do you know what would be best right now?" I ask finally, hoping to stir her back into action. "We should go about our daily business. We should get back to what we were doing before."

"How can you say that?" she asks. "A woman is dead!"

"She is with the Lord now."

"And is that enough for you?" she continues. "Do you not want to know why she was abandoned? Do you not wonder how she came to die up there, and how nobody thought to go and look for her?"

"The police will -"

"The police will close the case as quickly as they can," she says, interrupting me. "Do you think they have time to investigate an old death, especially one where there is no sign of foul play?" She pauses. "Especially one where the victim was so hated by everyone in the village."

"I understand your concern," I say calmly, "but Lizzy, you must listen to me. No good will come of histrionics. We have a duty to perform. I have a sermon to write, and you have a church to clean. People are coming tomorrow for the first service here in more than two years. The circumstances might be a little strained, but in this time of war we must all do out duty. Do you not see that?"

She pauses, before sniffing back tears and getting to her feet. She wipes her nose on a handkerchief, and then she straightens the front of her dress before heading to the door. Her steps are shuffling, as if she might at any moment collapse, and when she gets to the door she immediately reaches out as if to steady herself. Yet after a moment she turns to me, and I see to my relief that her tears have begun to dry.

"I shall get back to work," she tells me, her voice trembling just slightly now. "You are right. This is not the time to fall apart, is it? Not when there is so much to do."

Once she is gone, I sit at my desk and resume my work on the sermon. I must confess, I look out the window at one point and watch the cemetery, and I see several locals walking past the church. They glance this way; perhaps they see me, perhaps they do not, but I imagine they have all heard by now that Judith Prendergast's body has been found. It is to be hoped that some degree of relief will now spread throughout the village, and indeed I quickly resolve to add such a message into my first sermon.

I am sure that Judith Prendergast would want her death, however tragic it might have been, to be used for good.

CHAPTER SEVENTEEN

FROM UP HERE IN the bell-tower, one can see the entire village, and the view is rather spectacular. There are four arched openings, affording one a view to the north, south, east or west depending upon where one stands, but in all directions one sees rows of cottages stretching away toward either fields or a forest. This is the epitome of English country life, and I confess that – as I stand here now – I can think of no finer view in all the world.

Of course, I did not come back up here to admire the view.

Turning, I look back over at the spot where poor Judith Prendergast's body was found. As Doctor Sommersby warned me, and as I spotted myself earlier, there is indeed a dark patch where the body lay, specifically around the head area. As I walk over to take a closer look I see the sharp corner of the step onto which the woman seems to have fallen, and on which she must have hit her head. The corner is sharp and, I suppose, capable of causing death if struck at a certain angle.

But why was she left here?

Why did nobody in Briarwych care enough to come and check that she had left? Did the people of Briarwych really just assume that she was no longer here?

***

"I am done," Lizzy says as she reaches the doorway. "The church is clean for tomorrow's service. I have done my part in the preparation. I trust that your sermon is also ready?"

Having heard her approach, I take a moment to finish one more sentence in the journal, and then I set my pen down as I turn to her. Perhaps I am reading too much into things, but I believe I caught a slightly cold edge to her tone just now.

"I look forward to leading the service tomorrow," I tell her, "and I must thank you for your hard work. I put some money on the side for you, on the dresser. I hope that it will be sufficient."

She takes the money and quickly counts it.

"Are you alright?" I ask, even though I know I shouldn't.

She glances at me.

"You must have had quite a shock up there earlier," I continue. "Seeing that poor woman, I mean. I'm sorry if perhaps I seemed unduly harsh."

"I am fine," she replies. "You, too, must have had a shock. Are *you* alright?"

"Me?" Surprised, I furrow my brow. "Why, I am saddened, but I am perfectly fine. Thank you for asking."

"I wish I did not have to be paid at all for this," she says, as she slips the money into her pocket. "If I could afford to give the time for free, I would happily do so."

"Think nothing of it," I reply. "I would suggest that if you come every Monday and Thursday from now on, in the mornings, that would be sufficient."

She nods.

"And the hourly rate will remain the same," I add.

"You are very generous."

I smile, but still she does not leave. She seems to be hesitating, lingering for some reason, and after a moment I realize that perhaps she is not quite ready to go. In turn, I must admit that I like having her around.

"Is everything alright?" I ask. "Do you have anything to do for the rest of the day?"

"It's not that," she says. "To be honest, I live

alone, and sometimes..."

Her voice trails off.

"Plenty of quiet time for reading," I reply with an approving smile.

"Indeed." Still, she hesitates, and then she looks down at her hands. "I think it shall feel rather odd to be alone there tonight," she continues, "in the dark. I worry that my thoughts might turn to... Well, to matters I would rather not think about."

"The Lord will watch over you."

"I would rather not be alone."

"You are never alone with the Lord."

"I still see that face whenever I close my eyes," she says, as if her emotions of earlier are once again coming to the surface. "I cannot comprehend a night haunted by such images. How can I keep from having nightmares?"

"You must be strong," I tell her, not for the first time today.

"I don't suppose..." She takes a deep breath. "I don't suppose I could stay in one of the rooms here, could I? Just for one night?"

"I am afraid that would be out of the question," I tell her.

"I wouldn't make any noise, Father. I wouldn't cause you any trouble at all, I'd simply sleep in there very quietly."

"It's out of the question."

She opens her mouth to say something, but

then some inner resolve seems to make her realize that this would be inappropriate.

"I'm sorry," she mumbles, as she takes a step back and then retreats from view.

A moment later, I hear her hurrying out of the church. Turning, I look out the window and spot her making her way toward the gate, and then finally she disappears along the path that leads toward the village's edge. I do wish that I had been able to do more to console the poor girl, but I did all that was possible. And now, as I return my attention to tomorrow's sermon, I remind myself that I must help the whole village come to terms with this tragedy in their midst. I am quite sure that I can find some soothing words. I just need to work a little longer on what I am going to say.

CHAPTER EIGHTEEN

SUNDAY MORNING IS COLD and crisp. As I open the church's door, a full hour before the service is due to begin, I take a deep breath. I can feel the responsibility of my new position weighing on my shoulders, and after a few days' preparation I am ready to begin my role in this fine village. Today, a new chapter opens for Briarwych.

***

"And that is why we go forward with hope in our hearts," I continue, as I get to the final lines of my sermon, "and it is why, when this war is over, our fathers and brothers and sons will find that the same England they left, is still waiting right here for their return."

I pause for a moment, to allow those words to sink in. After a due period, I look up and out across the church, and from my position high in the pulpit I see the entire congregation. And I must confess that I feel a flicker of disappointment as I regard all those rows and rows of empty seats, with only five people having shown up this morning for my first service.

At the back, a man in a cap gets to his feet and hurries out, leaving just four people.

Even Lizzy did not think to attend this morning.

"Well," I say, forcing a smile in the hope of lifting the mood somewhat, "I hope that some comfort has been found in these words. Sometimes it's the small steps we must focus on, rather than the large. And perhaps one or two of you might share what you have heard today with others in the community, so that they too might benefit from some..."

My voice trails off.

The faces that stare back at me seem so bored, perhaps even mildly annoyed. They are so clearly waiting for me to release them, like children in a class at school, and I can only assume that they came today due to some sense of obligation. That, of course, is not particularly unusual, but it would appear that my sermon has done little to lift their spirits. Or their heads, in the case of one man near the back who seems to be struggling to stay awake.

"I hope you will all have a pleasant Sunday," I remark, "and I do hope to see all of you, and perhaps some fresh faces too, at next week's service."

With that, I take a step back, and the members of the congregation all understand the signal. They rise and, without speaking a word to one another, they all head toward the door. Once they are gone, I am left standing all alone in the pulpit, in complete and utter silence. I was not anticipating a huge gathering, nor am I the kind of man who demands adulation and endless praise for his words. Still, I had hoped that at least a few more people might come to meet me on my first Sunday in Briarwych. The weather is fine enough, so what kept them away from church?

Could it, perhaps, be a sense of guilt?

***

I hear the voices as soon as I round the corner, and then I spot the warmth of a fire burning in the windows of the Hog and Bucket public house. Evidently on this cold Sunday afternoon, the locals have gathered to talk and to laugh together, in defiance of the local licensing laws. As I make my way along the narrow street, I am minded to turn back, but the people in this place are members of the parish and I believe I must make contact as best I can.

Despite my reluctance, then, I reach the door to the public house and step inside, and I am immediately met by warmth from the fire that burns in the hearth.

In the same instant, however, the voices all stop and all the faces turn to me, and it is as if – by my mere presence – I have ended all the good times.

At the back of the group, somewhere near the bar area, a man clears his throat.

"Good afternoon, gentlemen," I say, smiling in an attempt to put them at ease. "I must confess, I did not intend to come in here, but I heard such raucous laughter that I felt I must investigate."

I wait, but nobody says a word.

"And as the service today was so sparsely attended," I add, "I thought, well, if the mountain won't come to Mohammad, then Mohammad..."

My voices trails off.

Perhaps that was not the finest example I could have used.

"Please," I continue, "don't mind me. Carry on as you were."

Again I wait, and again I am met merely by a sea of stares.

Heading to the bar, I find that several men step quickly out of my way. This is very polite and accommodating of them, although I cannot help but wonder whether they are in fact fearful of my very presence. Or, as I surmised earlier, they might be feeling a sense of collective guilt after hearing about the discovery of poor Miss Prendergast's body.

"A glass of water, please," I say to the barman, since I can think of nothing else that would be suitable.

"I'm sorry my wife and I didn't make it to your service this morning," a man next to me says, as a few of the others finally start talking nearby. "With the church having been shut for some time, I'm afraid we've taken to working on Sunday mornings, and we completely forgot. We'll be there next week, I promise. Well, we'll try, anyway."

"That's quite understandable," I reply. "I don't know if anybody has told you, but you missed a sermon on the value of community spirit, and on the importance of keeping hope alive."

"Sounds useful," he says, nodding not entirely convincingly. "I'll have to keep that in mind, Father."

He pauses for a moment.

"Did you talk about *her*?" he asks suddenly.

"I beg your pardon?"

"You know who I'm talking about. It'd seem odd if she didn't come up in your sermon, not after how she was found up in the bell-tower."

Turning to him, I think I do indeed sense a

flicker of guilt in his expression.

"Do you mean Miss Prendergast?" I ask.

He seems to almost flinch at the mere mention of that name.

"I didn't mention the deceased lady by name," I add.

"But that's not how you lot do it, is it?" he continues, and now he seems a little agitated. Behind him, several men are not talking but are most certainly eavesdropping on our conversation. "You're not direct about these things. You beat around the bush, but you always always draw judgment on people. You tell stories that are about how people should've behaved."

"Do you mean allegories?" I ask.

"I don't know what you call 'em, but I know you do it."

"I merely -"

"You're new here, Father Loveford," he adds, and now he seems positively anxious. "With all due respect, you don't know the whole story about that woman or about what she did to this village. I don't suppose you got the chance to talk to Father Perkins about her, did you?"

"Sadly, I never met Father Perkins."

"And have you heard from him? Do you know how he's doing?"

"I have no news to share," I reply, still feeling that it's too soon to mention the poor man's death. "I am sure that, no matter the circumstances, Father Perkins would have acquitted himself well, and that he dealt more than adequately with any difficulties in Briarwych."

"I'm sure you're sure of that," the man says. "You don't know what she was like, though. You don't know how she judged everyone, how she looked down on us all, how she told us we were all sinners just for the slightest little things. She told some of us we should whip ourselves, to beg forgiveness from the Lord!"

"That seems a little extreme," I admit.

"And she said forgiveness could only come through the flesh," he adds. "From blood. It was all about blood with her, and pain. I don't think she was all there, Father. Not in the head. I think there was something wrong with her."

"Might I remind you," I reply, "that you are talking about a woman who has died?"

"I know, but..."

His voice trails off, and then he looks past me, as if he's hoping for support from some of the other men.

"You'll have more people in your church next Sunday if you forget the whole matter," he continues finally, turning back to me. "If people aren't worried about having things mentioned, they'll be more inclined to show up. I can help spread the word, if it helps." He eyes me with a hint of suspicion. "You're *not* going to preach about her, are you? You wouldn't preach when you don't know the full story, I'm sure."

"And what is the full story?" I ask.

"There *is* no story. That's the full extent of it, to be sure. But the point is, nobody did anything wrong, and we don't want to be talked to as if we did. I'm sorry if I'm speaking out of turn, but I just thought you might like to know why there were so few people at your sermon today. Only two or three, I understand."

"A few more than that," I reply, taking a sip of water before setting the glass back down. "I want to thank you for your advice, and I shall certainly take all that you've said into consideration while I work on the sermon for next week. And of course, my work is about more than just a couple of hours on a Sunday. The church is open every day, and I would be happy for anyone to come and speak to me, about any matter that might be weighing on their minds."

"I doubt many people round here have anything weighing on their minds," he replies firmly. "Not much happens in Briarwych, you see. In fact, I'd go so far as to say that nothing at all has happened here for a very long time. And that's how we'd like to keep it."

"I -"

"That's how we'd like to keep it, Father," he

says again. "I hope you'll realize that."

I open my mouth to respond, but then I realize that several other men are watching us and listening to our conversation. And although I am loathe to jump to conclusions, I cannot escape the suspicion that I am being warned off.

CHAPTER NINETEEN

STEPPING BACK INTO THE CHURCH, I feel a sense of relief that I am no longer in that loud public house. The church might be cold and quiet, but sometimes one prefers to be alone. Indeed, as I make my way to my office, I feel rather glad that I have no further appointments for the rest of the day.

That encounter in the public house was distinctly unwelcoming, and has left me with the impression that nobody wants to talk about Judith Prendergast's death. Yet can the entire community really believe that they can ignore what happened?

Lost in thought, I reach the doorway that leads into my office, and then suddenly I stop. A woman is standing at my desk, silhouetted against the bright window. She's holding my sermon papers in her hands, looking through them, and then a moment later she turns and looks directly at me.

With a sigh of relief, I realize that it's just Lizzy.

"Oh, I'm sorry," she says, clearly a little surprised. She sets the papers down. "I know I shouldn't be in here."

She takes a moment to straighten the papers, making sure that they're neat and in line, and then she comes over to the doorway. She seems a little embarrassed as she slips past, but then she stops and turns back to me. As she does so, I see that there is a bruise on her left cheek.

"I heard your sermon earlier," she continues, "and I thought it was rather beautiful. I wanted to read some of the passages, that's all. To... relive the parts that I thought were particularly insightful."

"You heard the sermon?" I reply, shocked by the news. "I don't think I saw you in the congregation."

"I stayed out of sight, at the back. Behind the pillar, next to the door. I suppose that was foolish of me, really. I don't know why I did it, except that I didn't want to be a pain. I arrived a little late, you see, and then I saw how few people there were. I suppose I didn't want to be a distraction."

"I'm sure you would not have been," I tell her. "And if you had been, it would only have been in a positive manner."

"You really did give a most interesting sermon," she says. "It would have done a lot of people some good, if only they'd roused themselves and come to listen."

"That's very kind of you."

"And now I shall leave you in peace," she adds, taking a step back. "Again, I am sorry to have disturbed you."

She turns to leave.

"I have books," I say suddenly, rather surprising myself.

She turns back to me.

"There are books here, I mean," I continue. "I just thought, if you have nothing to do and you wish to read today, there are books here. You are welcome to take some away with you, or even to stay here and read. The church is very quiet, and you won't be disturbed." I pause, waiting for her to answer. "It was just a thought, that's all," I tell her. "I'm sure you have plenty to be getting on with today."

"You..."

She stares at me, as if the offer is an utter shock.

"You wouldn't mind?" she asks finally. "I know your work is important. I wouldn't be disturbing you, would I?"

"Of course not. In fact, I would be very pleased to have you here."

As soon as I have said those words, I realize that they make me sound rather forward. Lizzy is a remarkable young woman, and I do not wish to say anything that could be deemed inappropriate.

"It's entirely up to you," I add. "I'm sure there are plenty of other things that you could be doing on such a nice day."

"Oh, no," she says quickly, as if to cut off any further talk of alternatives. "I should greatly like to stay and read. I'll go into one of the other rooms, so as to not bother you." She hurries out of the room, before stopping and glancing back at me. "Thank you again, Father Loveford! You're too kind."

"Not at all," I reply, somewhat taken aback by her gratitude.

She runs off to the room with the bookcase, and I take a moment to reflect upon the fact that it might be pleasant to have somebody else around the place. And then, remembering my duties here at the church, I turn to my desk as I realize that I have another sermon to write.

***

"Let us not forsake such small pleasantries," I whisper, reading from my latest – rather poor, I must admit – attempt to write something useful, "and let us not -"

Before I can finish, I hear footsteps out in the corridor, and I turn to look over at the doorway. As I do so, I adjust my posture and sit up straight, then I take my glasses off in case they make me look too strict, or perhaps too old. Then, worried that without glasses I might appear vain, I set them back in place, while still waiting for Lizzy to reach the door. Then I glance at the candle that burns on my desk, set against the darkening evening outside, and I realize that the shadows might make me look older than my years. I suppose I *am* being vain.

The footsteps continue, but now it seems that they are heading toward the corridor's far end.

"Lizzy?" I call out. "Is everything alright?"

I wait, but she does not reply.

Supposing that she might be lost, I get to my feet and head to the door. As I look out into the corridor, however, I am surprised to find no sign whatsoever of Lizzy. At that exact moment, meanwhile, the footsteps come to an abrupt halt, leaving me standing in silence. I hesitate for a moment, before heading over to check one of the other rooms.

"Are you still reading?" I ask. "I was only -"

Stopping suddenly, I see that Lizzy is fast asleep in one of the armchairs, with an open book resting on her lap. She looks very peaceful, and I cannot help but smile as I see her closed eyes twitching slightly. She must be having a rather energized dream, as well she might since she appears to have been reading a collection of eighteenth century romantic odes.

The room is getting colder as evening advances, so I take a blanket from one of the stools and then I carefully set it over Lizzy's body, so as to ensure that she remains warm while she sleeps. And then, as I finish setting the blanket in place, I must confess that I hesitate and let my gaze linger on Lizzy's face for a little longer than is necessary.

She will make somebody a very fine wife one day. Indeed, she must be twenty-one if she is a day, so I wouldn't be surprised if she already has a suitor. Some lucky boy from the village is most likely already wooing her. Really, she should be out with him today, rather than reading old poems in a dusty church backroom. Certainly, she seems to have a wise head on her shoulders. I'm sure she understands that, when it comes to matters of the heart, the old-fashioned ways are often the best.

And then I notice the scratches on the nape of her neck.

I am loathe to look too closely, lest I be accused of informality, but there are several scratches on the back of Lizzy's neck. I peer a *little* closer, just enough to see that these scratches do indeed appear to run down beneath her collar, going out of view beneath the fabric. My first thought is that these must be the product of some self-punishment ritual, but I confess I have also heard of young girls – and boys – who occasionally self-harm for other reasons. Lizzy has always seemed to be a most carefree young lady, yet evidently she is in some ways deeply troubled. Yet what can I do, other than offer general comfort? It is certainly not my place to ask questions of a deeply personal nature.

I stare at her for a moment longer, before telling myself that I really should leave the room before I disturb her. Indeed, I need to contemplate my next course of action, because the scratches and the bruises make it quite clear that Lizzy is in need of guidance.

And then, just as I begin to turn, I once again hear footsteps out in the corridor. This time, the sound is quite clearly coming from the far end, so I head over to the doorway and look out, just as – once more – the footsteps suddenly stop. I wait, confused, trying to work out who might have entered the church. I am certain I would have heard somebody entering, as I have been working for several hours now in silence. It is simply inconceivable that anyone could have entered unnoticed.

A moment later, hearing a murmur, I turn and see that Lizzy has shifted slightly in the chair. She has not woken, but she mutters something unintelligible in her sleep.

Suddenly I hear a loud thump in the distance. Looking back out into the corridor, I am shocked to see that the church's main door has swung open, and that the inside handle has bumped against the wall. Hurrying over, I stop in the doorway and look out across the cemetery, but there is absolutely no sign of anybody near the church. I wait, in case somehow a visitor appears, but I suppose the failing evening light means that somebody must have simply slipped away into the shadows. Either that, or I am losing my mind.

"Is everything alright?"

Startled, I turn and see that Lizzy has emerged from the other room. With the blanket around her shoulders, she blinks away sleep.

"Father Loveford?" she continues. "You look a little pale."

"Of course," I stammer, "I merely..."

My voice trails off.

I merely *what*? I merely heard footsteps where there could be no footsteps? To admit that would be to invite ridicule, and – worse – to risk fanning the flames of this ridiculous ghost story. I must remain above all of that. I must lead by example.

"I merely noted that it is getting late," I say finally. "The lights must go off soon, and I am afraid I have an early start tomorrow, for I have to visit the RAF base in Littleton."

"I see," she replies. She stares at me for a moment, as if she does not quite understand, and then she nods. "Of course, you wish to retire for the night. I'm so sorry to have kept you up."

"You haven't kept me up," I say, as she hands me the blanket and steps outside. "Forgive my abruptness, you can of course stay and finish whatever you were reading."

"I shall come tomorrow morning to clean again, as arranged," she replies, and suddenly her tone seems much more formal than before. She barely even dares look at me as she takes a step back, and then she mumbles a goodbye before turning and hurrying away into the twilight. As she goes, she adjusts the back of her dress, as if perhaps she's worried that I might have seen the scratches.

"You can stay!" I tell her, but she does not respond.

I open my mouth to call after her again, but at the last moment I realize that there is no point. She doubtless has chores at home, and I have some work of my own to complete. With that, then, I swing the door shut, and then I pause for a moment as I realize how much I enjoyed having Lizzy here. Her presence seemed right somehow, and I must confess that there is a part of me that misses her already. I am sure that one day she will make some man a very good, very loving wife, provided she can recover from whatever malady it is that makes her harm herself. I fear that no man will want a wife who does such things. Perhaps this is why there is a hint of loneliness in her manner?

Heading through to my office, I resolve to finish work on my next sermon before I have to blow out the remaining candles for the night. The theme of this particular sermon shall be the need for forgiveness, and I can only hope that next time around I shall have rather more of a congregation than I managed to gather today. As I begin to write, however, I find my mind wandering back to the subject of Lizzy.

Forcing myself to stay focused, I return to the sermon. Yet once again I cannot help but think of Lizzy, and finally I lean back in my chair and look out the window, watching the darkening cemetery as I try to work out how I can possibly help the poor girl.

CHAPTER TWENTY

"FATHER!" A VOICE SHOUTS, as a fist continues to bang on the door. "Father Loveford, come quickly!"

Startled awake, I sit up in the darkness and listen as the banging goes on and on. For a moment I am not quite sure where I am, but then I feel the arms of the chair and I realize I must have fallen fast asleep. I instantly reach over and snuff out the candle, which – although it was almost dead anyway – nevertheless still burned in defiance of the blackout restrictions. How could I have been so foolish?

"Father Loveford, you must come!" the male voice continues, accompanied by further banging on the door. "Father Loveford, hurry!"

***

"It was awful, quite awful," Mr. Rose continues, clearly shaken as he leads me along the dark, winding street that runs into the heart of the village. "Didn't you hear her screams, Father?"

"I confess I did not," I reply, shivering slightly in the cold air. It is only a little after midnight, and I must admit that I am as yet not quite fully stirred from sleep.

"Here," Mr. Rose says, as we reach the outside of a terraced cottage, where several men and women are gathered in earnest conversation. "It's okay," he continues, pushing past them and then beckoning for me to follow. "Father Loveford has arrived, he'll see Edna now. You must make way for him. Move!"

The crowd parts, and I step toward the cottage's open front door. As I do so, I glance at the faces that are watching me, and even in the moonlight I can see expressions of suspicion and concern. Nobody greets me, nobody even seems particularly pleased by my arrival, so I simply nod an un-returned greeting at each of them before bowing my head and ducking under the low door that leads into the cottage.

"She's upstairs," Mr. Rose says, leading way by candlelight, already heading up to the cottage's upper floor. The stairs creak beneath his steps. "I'm so sorry to have roused you, Father Loveford, but poor Mrs. Canton is in a terrible state. She's rambling and sobbing, and nobody has been able to comfort her at all. We've all tried but, well, she hasn't been making much sense. Calling you is our last option."

"How gratifying," I murmur.

"You know what I mean, Father. We just didn't want to wake you, that's all."

"I shall do my best," I reply, having to duck once again as I find that these cottages all have such low ceilings and doorways. "Perhaps I can offer a prayer that will calm her soul."

As I say those words, however, I realize I can hear a woman's wailing voice coming from one of the bedrooms, and a moment later I look through and see a middle-aged woman with her head in her hands on a bed, while a man – presumably her husband – attempts in vain to console her. For a moment, the whole scene seems utterly cacophonous and out of control.

"Father Loveford is here," Mr. Rose says, as he stops and gesture for me to to through. "He'll know what to do."

"He's the last person we need!" a voice hisses.

"He might know what to do."

I hear a sigh.

"Give it a try," Mr. Rose continues. "Unless

you have any better ideas?"

There's a pause, and for a few seconds it seems as if I might be turned away.

"My wife is in a terrible state," Mr. Canton says finally, getting to his feet. He seems rather unsympathetic, as if he is mostly just annoyed by the whole disturbance. "Father, you can speak to her, if you think you can do any good. She's getting hysterical and that's most unlike her. I confess I slapped her once, in an attempt to get some sense into her, but she's utterly out of control. I've tried to talk some sense into her, but she won't listen."

"It's okay," I say, approaching Mrs. Canton as she continues to sob. "My dear lady, can you tell me what is the matter?"

"She's hysterical," her husband snaps. "I told you already."

"Might I ask what caused you to feel this way?" I ask the woman.

"Nothing, of course," her husband says, once again answering for her. "She just had a bad dream, that's all. Evidently she's not capable of determining dream from reality."

"Perhaps I might speak to your wife alone," I reply, turning to him. "If you don't mind, Mr. Canton."

He opens his mouth to answer, but then he simply sighs and heads out of the room. Something about the way he stomps along is enough to make me realize that I truly *am* the last resort in this situation.

"Whatever you wish," he says darkly. "This nonsense is entirely beyond the pale. A man should not be woken in his own home, by his own wife acting in this manner. Whatever is the world coming to?"

Once he is gone, I step over and swing the door shut, and then I turn to see that Mrs. Canton has at last looked up at me. Her eyes are filled with tears, and she is quite plainly in great distress, and after a moment I see that her hands are trembling as if she is extremely fearful. I wait a few seconds, hoping that she might volunteer some information, and then I step back around to the side of the bed. The lady is in her nightgown, so I am careful not to look at her too directly, for fear of seeming over-familiar. Indeed, she really should be wearing a dressing gown, but I suppose now is not the time to mention that.

Truthfully, I am not entirely sure how to begin this conversation.

"I saw her," she says suddenly, her voice shaking with fear.

"You saw who?" I ask.

"You know who. You must know." She makes the sign of the cross against her chest. "I saw her, Father. God save my soul, but I saw her face."

I am about to tell her that I have no idea, but

then in an instant I realize that perhaps this mess has something to do with all the stories about Judith Prendergast.

"What *exactly* did you see?" I ask cautiously.

She turns and looks over at the bedroom window, and I realize I can see true fear in her expression.

"What did you see?" I ask again.

"She was out there," she replies, still staring at the bedroom window. "I got up to use the bathroom. On my way back, I happened to look out and I saw her. I only looked out to check the weather, but then I spotted a figure down there on the road. For a moment I thought I was imagining it, but then I realized I could see her face. She was standing right down there in the road, staring straight up at me."

She pauses, and now there are tears in her eyes, and her bottom lip is trembling.

"Well, it's very dark out there," I point out. "Perhaps what you saw was somebody else."

"It was her!"

"Or a shadow."

"It was her!" she says firmly, turning back to me. "I knew the woman, Father! Not well, but I knew her! And I'm telling you, I saw her out there on the road tonight. Yes, it was dark, but there *was* some moonlight, and it was enough for me to see that face. That awful, staring, dead face. She was right outside!"

I hesitate, before stepping over to the window and peering out. Several men and women are still gathered outside the house, but there is certainly no sign of any spectral visitor. Nor indeed could there be, since such things are impossible.

"They found her body," Mrs. Canton continues. "What if, by removing it from the church, they stirred her spirit?"

"It seems that *something* has been stirred," I mutter, still watching the road for a moment before, finally, turning back to look at Mrs. Canton. "You say that you knew the poor deceased woman. Is it possible that the discovery of her body has woken some feelings?"

"You don't understand," she says, shaking her head.

"Perhaps, perhaps not," I reply. "You say that the dead woman was staring up at your window. Why would she be doing that? Why *your* window, and not any other?"

"I don't know what you mean, Father."

"What was your relationship to Miss Prendergast?"

"She hated the whole village," she continues. "Don't you get it? She hated us when she was alive, she thought us pagans and ingrates. Now in death, after the manner in which she passed away, she hates us even more."

"That sounds rather melodramatic," I point out.

"You do not believe in ghosts?"

"I believe in the ever-lasting soul."

"You don't believe that the dead walk the streets, seeking revenge for wrongs that were committed against them?"

"I don't believe in ghost stories, no."

"You would if you'd seen her tonight," she continues, with tears starting to run down her face. "Father, you'd believe if you'd seen her face like I saw her face."

"I think anyone who has committed a wrong," I reply, "would be best served by coming to confession at the church. Any guilty feelings – and I am not saying for one moment that anybody here has reason to feel guilty – but any guilty feelings are best aired, lest they should fester and cause disturbances." I pause for a moment. "A guilty soul can never sleep sound, Mrs. Canton. That's the thing about guilt. It wears us down."

I wait, half-expecting her to suddenly offer some kind of confession, but instead she stares at me stoney-faced. It is evident that my words are not having the desired impact, that she perhaps refuses to permit herself the necessary level of self-examination.

"You can go now, Father," she says

suddenly, her defenses now up. "I'm sorry you were disturbed, Father. It shall not happen again."

"If you need -"

"It shall not happen again," she says again, more firmly this time. "Goodnight, Father. Thank you for your efforts."

"If -"

"Goodnight, Father. Please send my husband in as you leave."

Realizing that there is not much more I can say to the woman, I turn and head toward the door.

"And Father," she adds, causing me to glance back at her. "You don't know what Judith Prendergast was like. Please, don't judge us for leaving her in that church. It's not our fault she didn't find a way out. And if you'd ever met the woman, you'd understand why we all just wanted to forget that she ever existed."

CHAPTER TWENTY-ONE

"PEOPLE ARE SPOOKED," Mr. Rose says as we make our way out of the house, and as the front door swings shut behind us. "Just when we were starting to forget about Judith Prendergast, now it's all been brought up again. Still, I'm sure we'll manage."

"I shall try to think of some way to address the matter again in this Sunday's sermon," I reply, turning to him. "Of course, for that to have any impact, I shall need people to actually come to the service."

"You must give them time."

"I do not intend to force them."

"It's late," Mr. Rose says, "and I don't know about you, but I have to be up early. Thank you for your time tonight, Father Loveford. I shall see you at the service on Sunday, if not before."

As I nod, and as he walks away, I turn to head back to the church. In that moment, however, I spot a shadowy figure standing nearby, seemingly watching me from next to a hedgerow. I must confess, I stop and feel a flicker of concern in my chest, before reminding myself that this most certainly cannot be the specter of the late, lamented Miss Judith Prendergast.

"Is Edna alright?" the woman asks suddenly, and as she steps forward I see that it is Mrs. Neill. "I heard her cry out from round the corner."

"I believe she will be fine," I tell her. "Might I ask about your son? Has he shown any signs of improvement?"

"He is comfortable. Thank you for your concern."

"And your other son? Is there any news from the front?"

Her face twitches slightly, as if the question troubles her.

"There is no news," she continues, her voice now sounding considerably tighter and more tense. "Which is good news, I suppose."

"If you change your mind," I reply, "I would be happy to join you in a prayer for his safety."

She shakes her head.

"Mrs. Neill, I -"

"I've told you, I can't," she says, taking a

step back, almost as if she is scared of me. "I can't pray, not when I know that by doing so I'll be damning some other mother's son. I just can't. Goodnight, Father."

With that, she turns and hurries off into the night before I have a chance to say anything more.

As her footsteps fade into the distance, I turn and make my way along the road that slopes gently uphill toward the church. I must confess that I am rather troubled by my continued inability to make inroads when it comes to the local population, but I suppose I should not be too harsh on myself. I have been here for less than a week, and I most certainly seem to have arrived in the midst of a difficult situation. The death of Judith Prendergast has evidently caused a great deal of trouble in Briarwych, and it will not be the work of a moment to unpick all of that and to settle the village's collective nerves.

For that to happen, they must face their collective guilt. And I do not feel that they are ready for that yet.

Reaching the churchyard, I step past the gate and make my way toward the door. As I do so, I cannot help but glance at the windows, which – although dark – are in some places picked out by patches of moonlight. I know that there is no truth to the stories of Miss Prendergast appearing at those windows, of course, yet still I keep my eyes on those open spaces as I approach. I suppose that I am trying to prove to myself that nothing is amiss, and sure enough I see nothing as I reach the door. The calm, ordered mind is not given to hysterical ghost stories.

Taking the key from my pocket, I reach for the lock, only to find that the door is slightly open. In a flash, I realize that I must have forgotten to lock it when I was hurrying out with Mr. Rose, although I am certain that I at least pulled the door shut. Now it is hanging partially open, and I feel a sense of concern in my chest as I push the door all the way and stare into the cold, pitch darkness of the church's interior. Truthfully, I can understand how a guilt-laden soul might, in such circumstances, begin to imagine whispers coming from these shadows.

I wait, but all I hear is the sound of my own breath.

Stepping inside, I cannot help but wonder whether somebody might have taken advantage of the open door. Then again, I can't imagine that anybody here in Briarwych would do such a thing. Nevertheless, I wait for a moment longer before gently shutting the door, and then I slip the key into the lock and make sure that the church is properly secure. Then I turn and make my way along the dark corridor, heading toward my bedroom. As I do so, I pass the door that leads into the church's main section, but I do not look directly through as I walk.

And then I stop, as I realize that – in the corner of my eye – I spotted a figure standing silently at the altar.

I hesitate for a moment, before forcing myself to step back and take another look. This time, there is nobody to be seen, but I still look around and watch the rows of pews in case a figure might suddenly appear.

I open my mouth to call out, but I am sure I would sound terribly foolish were I to indulge these foolish imaginings. Yet at the same time, I cannot dismiss my fears out of hand, for the figure – though seen only in a flash – was very clear and very distinct against the church's pale stone walls, and I am quite sure that I saw the outline of a woman. Finally, unable to help myself, I clear my throat.

"Hello?" I call out. "Is anybody here?"

I wait, and then I make my way along the aisle, walking between the pews and looking around in case I spot any hint of movement. When I reach the altar, and the spot where the woman was standing, I turn and look back the way I just came, yet still there is nobody in sight.

"I am quite alright with you being here," I continue, wondering whether perhaps some fearful local is worried about getting into trouble. "Please, there is no reason to hide, no reason at all."

I wait, and then I realize that perhaps it would help to add a little humor.

"I do not bite," I say.

Silence.

"Lizzy, it's not you, is it?" I add, and I must confess that I should like to see her face at this juncture. "Did you perhaps come back for more books?"

I hesitate for a few more seconds, before starting to make my way back along the aisle. I know what I saw, but at the same time it is also quite clear that nobody else is here. I suppose that all this activity at such a late hour must simply have left me rather susceptible to suggestion, and I tell myself that I must remain alert to any such failings. Still, as I reach the corridor, I cannot help but look over my shoulder and glance one more time at the altar, just to make absolutely certain that the figure has not reappeared.

It has not, so I head to my bedroom, before taking a quick detour into the office.

Heading to the desk, I reach out for a notebook. As I do so, however, I spot a crumpled ball of paper on the desk, and I know for certain that there was no such ball when I left. Reaching down, I pick up the piece of paper and start to pull it open, and I feel a shudder in my chest as I see that this is the page upon which I have been writing out my upcoming sermon on the subject of forgiveness.

Looking over my shoulder, I listen for a moment to the silence of the church.

Were I a weaker-minded man, I must at this juncture come to believe that some spirit took issue with my sermon and demonstrated its displeasure. Alternatively, I might allow myself to believe that the sermon was spoiled by an interloper who crept into the church. Refusing to believe either thing, however, I realize with a sigh that I simply *must* have screwed the piece of paper up earlier, and now for some reason I do not remember doing this at all. Yet I must have done it, because there is no other possibility, so I straighten the piece of paper out and set it back down, so that I might return to it at some point tomorrow.

As I do so, I see that the sheet has not merely been screwed up. Scratches have been ripped straight down through the page, as if somebody wanted to destroy the sermon entirely. A sermon, I might add, that is all about forgiveness.

CHAPTER TWENTY-TWO

Six weeks later

"BUT WHAT I TRULY hope you will take from today's service," I continue, despite the increasing dryness of my mouth, "is the sheer joy of worship. For it is this joy that represents God's gift to us, and which lights our way no matter how dark the night."

I pause for a moment, staring down at those final words, and then I look out across the congregation.

Mr. Hopkins clears his throat.

Miss Frazer stares at me with a friendly, perhaps slightly sympathetic smile.

Lizzy sits eagerly, as if she has listened to – and absorbed – every word.

And that is the extent of it, since these three

are the only people who came this week. I am accustomed to low turnouts here in Briarwych, and indeed I have still not managed to attract more than eight people in any one week, but three is a particular disappointment, although I force a smile in an attempt to hide this disappointment. I had hoped that I might be building some momentum, yet evidently that is not the case.

"Thank you once again for coming," I say, "and I do hope to see you all again next Sunday. Perhaps with some friends and family members along. Feel free to invite anyone you can think of. We have, as you can see, plenty of free seats."

An awkward silence ensures for a few seconds, but Mr. Hopkins finally gets to his feet. This seems to be the signal for which Miss Frazer was waiting, for she swiftly gets to her feet and follows him toward the door, as I make my way down from the pulpit and walk over to the altar. There, I stop for a moment to fold my sermon away, while trying to get my head around the fact that I continue to attract so few people to the church.

"You mustn't lose hope," Lizzy says, and I turn to see her coming over to join me. "Your sermons are wonderful, Father Loveford. It's just going to take time, that's all."

"Indeed," I reply, once again forcing a smile.

"You're worried," she continues. "I can see it in your eyes."

"Of course I'm not worried," I tell her, although I know that she sees through the lie. "Although it is natural for one to wonder whether one is performing at one's best, when one seems to attract so little interest."

I pause for a moment, feeling most uncomfortable.

"I should go to my desk," I add finally, turning to walk away. "Tomorrow is my trip to London, and first I must contemplate matters."

"Don't."

I turn to her.

"Don't what?"

"Don't start to doubt yourself," she continues, hurrying around as if to block my way. "Please, Father Loveford, you must recognize that the problem is not you. The problem is this place. You're doing far better than anybody else would manage in this position, and you must simply give it time."

"That's very kind of you to say," I reply, stepping past her, "but I am not -"

"Don't give up," she adds, suddenly putting a hand on my arm to stop me.

Startled by the contact, I look down at her hand, which she quickly withdraws.

"I'm sorry," she says, "I didn't mean to... I mean, you must forgive me. I shouldn't have been so forward."

"After six weeks," I reply, "it is evident that my methods are not working. I have a train journey to London tomorrow, and I intend to use that time for some quiet, sober reflection. If there is something I can change, then I must change it. The people of Briarwych deserve a priest who can cater to their needs."

"I have faith in you," she says, keeping her eyes fixed on me.

"And that is good to know," I tell her. "Would that some of the others in the village might feel the same. And now, if you will excuse me, I must go and check that my papers for tomorrow are in order."

"Their guilt is not your fault," she says earnestly. "They did something terrible, all of them together. They didn't bother to check to see if Miss Prendergast was okay. Now they don't want to admit this, so they hide away and they think they can ignore what they did. But you can forgive them, can't you? If only they come to you and ask?"

"I can certainly help them," I reply, "but they are the ones who must forgive themselves. And in order to do that, they must first admit to what they have done."

***

Later that evening, as I click my case shut in the

dying light of the office, I cannot help but think back to that earlier conversation with Lizzy. She seemed so keen to reassure me, to tell me that I am doing the right thing, yet in my heart of hearts I am already beginning to worry that my ambitions here at Briarwych are fated to failure. If I cannot even get people to come to one of my services, how am I ever to reach out and make them listen?

Once I am certain that everything is ready for the morning, I head to the door and step out into the cemetery. The sun is starting to set, and soon all lights will have to be out, but for now the village looks extremely calm and peaceful. Indeed, I almost feel as if my efforts here are disturbing what was already a comfortable life for the locals. It is almost as if they do not need the church.

Although I know I should get an early night, I decide to take a short walk. Wandering out through the gate, I head along the sloping road that leads down into the center of the village, and in truth I am glad of the shadows that make me less obvious. The road is empty anyway, but I feel as if my very presence is an intrusion, and I worry that the people here would not be particularly overjoyed if they were to encounter me here. In fact, as I reach the end of the road, I am already starting to think that I should head back to the church.

And then I hear a commotion in the distance, raised voices and some degree of disagreement.

Stepping around the corner, I look along the next road and immediately see that the lights are still on in the public house. That is where the noise is coming from, and I must confess that I take a few more steps in the direction of the window, keen to determine what might be causing the disruption. It sounds as if there is an argument taking place inside, and as I get closer I see that there are plenty of people inside. Finally, just as I am about to take another step, the front door opens and I instinctively step back into the shadows as a figure emerges from the building.

Stopping, the figure holds the door open and looks back inside, and even in the low light I immediately recognize her face.

"You're all wrong!" Lizzy shouts back into the public house, her tone filled with a kind of anger that I never would have imagined she might possess. "You stand around in here night after night, patting each other on the back, telling each other that you're doing the right thing. The truth is, you can't any of you see the wood for the trees!"

"Go on, Lizzy!" a harsh, drunken voice cries out from inside. "Be off with you! No-one wants to hear this, not now!"

"You know I'm right!" she sneers. "Maybe if you actually went to one of his services, just one, you'd see it for yourselves, but you're too scared, aren't you? That's what it boils down to in the end!

Fear! You're a bunch of cowards, huddled together to make each other feel better and -"

"Go home!"

"- and never daring to actually face up to what it is that you did! The Lord knows, though. You can't hide from him. He sees everything you do, including your cowardice. And if any of you actually dared go to one of Father Loveford's services, then he'd see that too, and he'd see that maybe – just maybe – you're willing to repent for your sins! Until that day, though, you might as well stand around in this place and get drunk!"

"Now listen, young lady," a voice says, "you're no -"

Slamming the door shut, Lizzy steps back and puts her head in her hands for a moment. She seems to be crying, and a moment later she turns and hurries away along the darkening street.

I make to go after her, but something holds me back and within a couple of seconds she has entirely disappeared from view around the far corner.

Turning, I look into the public house and see that the locals are once again talking loudly and merrily at the bar, as if they're amused by everything that Lizzy just said. A moment later the laughter builds to a crescendo, and somewhere in the throng of voices I hear some light-hearted jokes about how Lizzy should get back to the kitchen and stop bothering men while they're drinking. I want to go storming in there and to tell these oafs that they'd be better off listening to her, but once again I restrain myself. I am in no position to go making enemies here in Briarwych, and that – perhaps more than anything else – is why my role here is becoming increasingly untenable.

I step back, retreating from the window, and then I turn and start making my way back toward the church. Tomorrow I journey to London for a couple of nights. I have told Lizzy that I am merely going to complete some business, but I have not been entirely honest with her. In truth, I have another aim entirely.

CHAPTER TWENTY-THREE

THE ENGLISH COUNTRYSIDE FLASHES past as I sit staring out of the train window. Occasionally I spot a distant village or hamlet, sometimes even a church spire, and I am reminded of all the great traditions that keep this country alive. Each of those spires marks a church, and in most of those churches there will be a priest – a man very much like myself – who provides comfort and guidance to his flock.

Yet as the train continues to hurtle toward London, I cannot escape a feeling of great inadequacy, as I reflect upon the fact that after almost two months I have helped nobody at all in Briarwych. I am failing in my duty.

***

"It's so good to see you, Lionel," Bishop Carmichael says as he shuffles slowly across his office. "Things haven't been the same around here since we punted you off to that little shire in the middle of nowhere. I'd almost go so far as to say that your presence has been greatly missed. *Almost*."

At that little joke, he chuckles.

"You are too kind," I reply, as I see that – as usual – Bishop Carmichael's desk is absolutely covered in piles upon piles of paperwork. How the man ever gets anything done, I cannot imagine. "I am sure that everything is in hand here."

A bus roars past the building, rattling the windows; a useful reminder, were a reminder needed, that even in wartime London remains a loud place. Why, if German bombers could be guided to their targets by sound alone, this great city would surely be blown to oblivion every single night. How I miss the quiet solitude of the English countryside.

"So how go things in your new parish?" Bishop Carmichael asks as he takes a seat. Reaching out, he picks up one of his files, although in the process he sends several others sliding off and clattering to the floor. "Oh dear."

"Let me," I reply, heading over and reaching down, then setting the files back on the desk, hopefully a little less precariously this time.

"What's the name of your new place again?" he continues. "Bowelwych, something like that? Bowelford?"

"Briarwych," I remind him, as I get back to my feet, "and I must say, it -"

Before I can finish, more files slither off the desk and land at my feet. Crouching down, I pick them back up and put them onto the desk. As I do so, I see that these particular files pertain to some land near Coventry. Truly, Bishop Carmichael's work covers a vast area.

"Briarwych," Bishop Carmichael muses, as if he hadn't even noticed the paperwork that keeps raining off the sides of his work-space, "that's right. Yes, I remember now. Perkins' old stomping ground. Been vacant for a while before you took the job on, from what I remember. I bet the chaps and chapesses of that parish are glad to have someone around again, aren't they?"

Unsure as to how I might truthfully answer, I hesitate for a moment. I could say nothing and pretend that my work in Briarwych is an outstanding success, but that would be a lie, not least to myself. I must be honest and confess my failings.

"Actually," I say cautiously, "I must confess that my reasons for coming here today are not entirely positive. I am reluctant to trouble you, but I have been in Briarwych for some time now and I cannot say that things are going entirely well. In fact, I have barely managed to attract more than half a dozen parishioners to any one of my sermons, and matters are showing no signs of improvement. I am beginning to think that -"

Suddenly some more papers come crashing down.

"Beginning to think what?" Bishop Carmichael mutters, barely managing a glance at the mess before looking back at a book on the desk. "Did something fall?"

"You have said it yourself in the past," I point out, as I crouch down and once again start gathering the papers back up, "that sometimes a man is simply sent to the wrong place at the wrong time. I know you had trouble filling the vacancy after Father Perkins' departure, and I do not for one moment wish to cause difficulties at what must be an awkward time, but it is becoming clear to me that I might not be the man for this particular job."

Reaching up, I start carefully balancing the papers on the desk. A couple immediately slide back down, hitting me in the face, although I manage to put them back into place without letting them hit the floor again. As I do so, I see that these particular papers refer to parishes in the Kent and East Sussex regions.

Getting to my feet, I take a moment to brush

myself down.

"I was wondering," I continue, "whether there might be a man who is more suitable to this particular task."

"Picking up papers?"

"Tending to the flock at Briarwych."

He looks up at me.

"Are you saying that you're giving up, Father Loveford?" He adjusts his spectacles. "Are you, as they say, throwing in the proverbial towel?"

"Not *giving up*," I reply, trying to choose my words with care, "more... I suppose I'm trying to think about what's best for the people of that little village. If I'm not meeting their needs, then perhaps there is somebody else who would be better suited to the task."

Another file almost falls off the desk, but this time I am quick enough to catch it in time. Looking down, I see that these files concern some parishes in Cornwall, around the Falmouth and Helston area.

"And is this your sole reason for coming to London today, Father Loveford?" Bishop Carmichael asks, removing his spectacles as he leans back in his chair. The leather creaks beneath his weight. "To confess your so-called failure and to beg for somebody else to take your burden? You wish to be relieved of your duty?"

"My original plan was to collect a few cases

that I left behind when I departed," I reply, "but as it happens, the timing is... I mean, it would seem to me that somebody else might gain the truth of the local population in Briarwych. For whatever reason, they have taken against me and I see no way to repair the damage."

I wait, but he merely continues to stare at me.

"I have failed," I add finally, hoping to underline my point and to make it clear that something must be done. "There, I said it. I have failed in Briarwych, and I am humbly requesting a new placement."

Again I wait, and again he simply watches me.

"I am truly sorry," I continue, "for having not lived up to your faith in me."

I wait.

No answer.

"Perhaps I would be better served here, in administration," I suggest.

Again, he simply stares at me.

"Anything, really," I add, starting to feel a little desperate. "Anything except going back to that place."

I wait.

He stares at me.

And then, finally, he looks down at his papers and mumbles something that I don't quite make out.

I wait.

"I'm afraid," I say after a moment, "that I didn't quite -"

"I said it's quite out of the question," he grumbles. "You're no quitter, Loveford. I won't allow it."

"But if it's in the best interests of the -"

"And they need you at the RAF base," he says suddenly, cutting me off. "That's the truth of it, Loveford. After the rigmarole with Perkins a while back, nobody was particularly keen to send another man to Briarwych. But the brave men at the RAF base need a priest, and they won't have one permanently stationed at the airbase. A compromise is to have somebody at Briarwych, but in all honesty it's the airbase that needs you."

"But if -"

"So don't worry too much about the village," he continues. "Be ready for when they need you out at the airbase, and in the meantime try not to cause too much trouble among the local population. That's your job out there, Loveford, and I'm sure you can manage it. Carry on with your services, speak to those who wish to be spoken to, and make the best possible use of the rest of your time."

"Is that it?" I ask. "I am just to sit around, on call for the airbase?"

"Some people would kill for such an easy

assignment," he replies, as he puts his spectacles back on and returns his attention to his notes. "And it *won't* be easy, not always. Now don't rock the boat, dear chap. If you don't have anything else to talk about, I'm afraid that I'm terribly busy at the moment. In case you hadn't noticed, there *is* still a war going on."

I open my mouth to ask him again for a transfer, but I know Bishop Carmichael well enough to understand that when his mind is made up, there is no use trying to dissuade him. Instead, then, I take a step back, only for more files to immediately slip to the floor. I almost leave them there, but then I reach down and pick them up, only to hesitate as I see that one of the files bears the names of my predecessor, Father Perkins. A moment later, I see several sealed envelopes slipping out of one side, with Bishop Carmichael's name written on the front of each in the same ragged handwriting.

Taking out the small bundle of letters, I see that they are indeed all addressed in a scrawled text. A postmark shows that all of these letters were sent from somewhere named Huntingford Asylum in the EC1 part of London.

"Might I ask what these pertain to?" I say, turning to Bishop Carmichael.

"Eh?" He looks at the file, and then he rolls his eyes. "Oh, that nonsense. There's a chap at some lunatic asylum who keeps writing to us, claiming to have been in the army with Perkins. He wants somebody to go and see him, he says he was with Perkins when the poor chap bought it."

"And *has* anybody been to see him?"

"Of course not," Bishop Carmichael scoffs. "The man's obviously a lunatic, else why would he be in an asylum? I don't have time to talk to lunatics. I have enough trouble with Archbishop Clercy."

Slipping one of the opened letters out, I glance at the name at the bottom.

"Francis Townley," I whisper, before putting the file back onto the table and taking a step back.

"Now clear off, Loveford," Bishop Carmichael continues. "No offense, but I've got to finish this letter to the bloody Prime Minister. I can't personally stand the man, so it's all I can manage to hold a polite tone." He glances at me one more time. "And get back to Briarwych as soon as you can, eh? Those poor lads at the airbase will need you at some point, you know. When they do, you'll understand the real reason why you have to be down in that neck of the woods."

I know that he's right. And yet, as I leave his office, I cannot help but think about my predecessor in Briarwych. I would dearly like to get Father Perkins' opinion on the village, but of course that is impossible. Perhaps, however, a visit to Huntingford Asylum might be in order.

CHAPTER TWENTY-FOUR

"THANK YOU AGAIN FOR storing these cases," I say to Mrs. Wellesley as I pick up the two suitcases that, for the past six weeks, have resided here in my old boarding house on Jamaica Road. "I hope they weren't too much of an inconvenience."

"Not at all, Father," she replies with a smile. "It's good to see you again, although I wish you could stay for longer. Are you really taking the train back already this evening?"

"I am," I tell her. "At six o'clock, as it happens."

"I thought you were staying a night or two?"

"My plans have changed. I must get back to Briarwych, and the last train is at six."

"That's a fair few hours away," she points out. "Are you sure you don't have time to sit and enjoy a cup of tea before you leave?"

"That's a very kind offer," I reply, "and ordinarily I would be pleased to accept, but I have one other visit I must make while I am here. It's a place quite close to the train station, so it won't be too far out of my way. A last-minute addition to my itinerary, you might say."

***

"Go on, get out of here!" a man screams, as a young boy races along the street with a package under his arm. He runs so fast, he almost slams straight into me, and I have to take a step back to avoid him.

In doing so, however, I almost walk straight into the path of a car, which beeps its horn to warn me. I step back onto the pavement, momentarily dazzled by the sound of so much rushing about, and then I step over to the high, wrought iron gate that has been my target as I have struggled to cross this busy thoroughfare.

Above, a large sign bears the name of Huntingford Asylum. Beyond that sign there stands a large, formidable gray-stoned building with bars on its windows. Even now, standing here with my suitcases in my hands, I cannot help but feel that I can sense the anguish and despair emanating from within. Even in a time of warfare, what kind of wretched soul ends up in a place like this?

***

"We really don't usually allow visitors outside of regular hours," the doctor says as he stops at a door and fishes some keys from his pocket, "but we can of course make an exception for a man of the cloth. Besides, poor Frank doesn't get many visitors. Well, none, to tell the truth. I suppose it might be good for him."

With that, he unlocks the door and pulls it open, and then he peers into the cell.

"Are you feeling alright today, Frank?" he asks, as I hear a faint coughing sound coming from inside the room. "Somebody's here to see you. A man from the church, as it happens, so make yourself presentable."

From inside the cell, there now comes a ruffling sound.

In the distance, metal is banging against metal, and voices are calling out. Every few minutes I hear some far-off cry, and it is clear that this place is filled with the most troubled of souls. Would that I had time to visit them all, to perhaps offer them a little understanding and kindness, and to listen to their complaints.

"Put your britches on," the doctor says, still looking into the cell. "That's right. Good man."

I wait, once again hearing a rustling sound. I

can smell something foul, too, and I am beginning to wonder whether the inmates here at Huntingford are being kept in an entirely humane manner.

"That's better," the doctor continues, before turning to me. "Frank's completely harmless. He's just traumatized by his experiences in the war, that's all. They keep asking if he can go back to service, but there's simply no way. Some men get broken out there, you see, and there's nothing much that can be done for them. Perhaps it's a kind of weakness, something baked into their souls." He gestures for me to go into the cell. "Please, Father Loveford. Take all the time that you need. He's not wanted for anything else."

I nod, before stepping forward and making my way to the doorway. When I look into the cell, however, I'm shocked to see a man crouched on the bed, feverishly spitting onto his hands and then trying to neaten his unruly hair. The light is low and flies are buzzing around.

"Don't mind the smell too much," the doctor whispers to me. "Come to the desk when you're done, and somebody will show you out."

I hesitate, horrified by the conditions.

"I promise you he's harmless," the doctor adds. "I wouldn't leave you with him otherwise. If he *wasn't* harmless, he might actually be some use to someone."

I thank him, and then – as he walks away – I

remain in the doorway and look at Mr. Frank Townley. Despite the fact that he looks rather dirty, he's clearly attempting to tidy himself up, although his efforts are for the most part rather useless. Still, it's good to see that the man retains a few standards, even if the look in his eyes is somewhat maniacal.

"Hello Francis," I say, trying to strike a friendly tone as I wave a few of the flies away. "My name is Father Lionel Loveford, and I -"

"What do you want from me?" he stammers, his voice barely rising above a series of grunts and groans. "I ain't done nothing wrong. I don't need to confess. Just trying to earn a crust, that's all."

"I can of course hear any confession you might want to make," I tell him, "but that is not why I am here." I pause, before taking a step into the foul-smelling cell. "It is my understanding that you have written a series of letters to the office of Bishop Carmichael, on the subject of the late Father David Perkins. If you -"

"Have you come about him?" Francis snaps.

"Well, I don't know whether you're aware, but Father Perkins tragically died in Ypres a short while ago. He was -"

"You don't know whether I'm aware?" he gasps, as his eyes open wide with shock. A moment later, he starts laughing. "You don't know whether I'm aware?" he chuckles. "That's priceless, absolutely priceless." He slams a hand against the side of his bed. "I was there, you daft sod. Forgive the language, Father, but I was there when old Davey died. I was in Ypres with him, I saw the -"

Suddenly his face twitches, and it takes a moment for him to regather his composure.

"I was with him," he continues. "Day in, day out, for the last six months of his life. I knew him better perhaps than any other man."

"I hope he was of comfort to you," I reply, before swatting away a fly that briefly landed on my forehead.

Nearby, human excrement is piled in the corner of the cell.

"It wasn't me who needed comforting," Frank says. "Davey wasn't a happy man, Father. He was terrified, always jumping at the slightest provocation. Restless days, sleepless nights. There's no wonder he couldn't cope, but there was no way he ever wanted to talk about it much. He was -"

He flinches, as his face once again twitches. He tries to wave away a fly, but already several more are crawling over his face.

"He was a good man," he continues, before spitting one of the flies away from his lips, "but he was haunted. Tell me, how did the official report say that he died?"

"I believe some mention is made of a booby-trap in a house. A house that had recently been occupied by some Germans."

"And what exactly do you think happened in there?" Francis asks.

"I imagine he was very unfortunate," I reply. "I can only pray that his death was quick and painless. I am sure that the Lord would have ensured that it was so."

At this, Frank chuckles.

"Was it not so?" I ask, feeling a flicker of concern. "A bomb would be quick, would it not?"

"You're just like the rest of 'em," Francis says, shaking his head as if he can't quiet believe what he's hearing. "You don't get it, do you? You didn't believe him, not all the times he told you about it."

"I'm afraid that you're losing me," I tell him, and now I am feeling a little frustrated. As I wave more flies away from my face, I am beginning to wish that this man could say his piece and then let me leave. I know that is not very Christian of me, but truly the stench in here is overwhelming. "Could you please explain why you have been so frequently writing letters to Father Carmichael? Obviously you have something to say, man, so say it."

"He said she was there," he explains. "He was always seeing her, he said he couldn't escape, but people thought he was mad. They thought he was seeing things, on account of the stress." He leans forward, then back again, as if he's highly agitated. "That's what people need to know, you see? It was going on for months, he kept seeing her, and no-one took him seriously."

"I'm rather afraid that you've lost me," I reply. "Who was Father Perkins seeing?"

"He said she was following him around. He said even out there, she'd found him. He caught glimpses of her, and over the months he slowly became more and more nervous. Sometimes I'd be talking to him, and I could tell he was seeing her in the room, 'cept I couldn't see her at all. At first I was like the others, I thought he was just a bit doo-lally, but over time I began to realize that maybe there was more to it. Occasionally I even heard him begging her to leave him alone. Sobbing, he was, and putting his hands on the sides of his head. He'd be doing that all night, every night. The last week before he died, I don't reckon he got any sleep at all."

Suddenly he does the same, clutching his own head and starting to rock back and forth.

"Like this!" he cries out. "Begging her, just begging her! Leave me alone! Leave me alone! Like that!"

"I'm not sure what this has to do with anything, but..."

"Go away, Judith!" he shouts. "I didn't do anything to you! Go away! Go away! Go away!"

"Judith?" I hesitate for a moment,

wondering whether this might all be a coincidence. A moment later a fly lands in my left ear, and I hurriedly wave it away. "Are you absolutely *certain* that Judith was the name he mentioned?"

"Over and over," he says, still rocking for a few seconds before finally leaning back, breathless, against the wall and staring at me with fear-filled eyes. "It got worse as time went by. Eventually it was happening several times a day, like she wouldn't leave him alone. He tried to ignore her, he tried everything. By the time we got to Ypres, he was a broken man. Sometimes I even heard him at night, in our barracks, weeping and begging her to leave him alone. One time I even..."

His voice trails off.

"You even what?" I ask cautiously.

I wait, watching as a fly crawls up his chin. Frank's lips part slightly, and the fly crawls inside, and the man does not seem to react in any way whatsoever.

"You even what?" I ask again, starting to feel repulsed and frustrated in equal measure. "What, Frank?"

"I don't know if I really did see her or not," he replies, with a hint of wonder in his voice, "but I saw *something*. It was so dark, and so late at night. I was half asleep, but Davey was whispering and begging to be left alone, and I glanced over. Maybe it was nothing, but for a moment I swear I saw a woman leaning over his bunk. Dressed in gray she was, with long hair hanging down, and she had a hand reached out toward the side of his face. Such a pale hand, pale and thin. Then I blinked and she was gone, but Davey was still terrified."

"You were exhausted," I remind him. "You said it yourself, it was late at night and you were tired."

"The next day we were clearing houses in Ypres," he continues. "We got to this one house, and we found a booby-trap in one of the rooms. Well-hidden, it was, but me and Davey we saw it. We were good at that sort of thing, Jerry didn't get much past us. Davey said he'd forgotten his cutters. I told him I saw him put them in his pocket, but he swore he'd left them outside. He asked me to go and get them. Well, I didn't want to argue with him, so I went to take a look. As I was leaving, I thought I heard him talking to that woman again, but I didn't pay much attention. I went outside and checked the kit-bag, and of course I was right, the cutters weren't there at all. And then..."

Again, his voice trails off.

I wait, while still trying to convince myself that this is all nonsense.

"And then the whole bloody top floor went off," he adds finally. "It must've been the trap we'd found. The official report said Davey maybe tagged it by accident, but I knew Davey and I can tell you he'd never have done that."

"So what are you suggesting?" I ask.

"I've written to so many people, begging them to listen," he continues. "Even the church ignores my letters. But people have to know, Davey wasn't careless. I reckon he sent me out on a wild goose chase, just to make sure I was safe. And then, to finally stop that woman haunting him, he..."

He pauses, and then he swallows hard. There are tears in his eyes now.

"It's the only explanation," he adds. "Davey Perkins would never have tripped that wire and got him blown up. Not unless he intended to. Not unless he thought it was the only way to get away from her always whispering in his ear." He shudders for a moment. "I know how ghosts work, Father. The first twenty-four hours are the most important. Most dead spirits fade away in that time, but a few linger, especially if they're in some way trapped in the place where they died. Some, the really strong ones, can reach out further on occasion. Like she did to Davey, to push him into..."

His voice trails off, and his eyes widen with horror.

"Are you suggesting that he killed himself?" I ask.

He shudders, and then he spits out the mangled corpse of a little fly, letting it fall to the floor. Then he does the same again, and he opens his mouth enough for me to see that his stained and rotten teeth are covered in black stains and in patches of little torn-off legs.

"That's not possible," I continue, as Frank starts laughing. "I'm afraid you're like the others, you're allowing your imagination to run riot at the expense of all reason. It's not -"

Suddenly his laugh bursts into a full-throated howl, and he starts rocking back and forward once again.

"You're not seeing things clearly at all," I tell him, hoping to get through to the man even as I have to swat away more flies. "Please, you have to be sensible about this. I demand that you quieten down and listen to me."

Still he howls with laughter, his cries getting louder and louder until I step back against the bars of the cell. It's almost as if the man is screaming now.

"You have to listen," I continue, although now my voice is trembling and I can barely hear my own words over the sound of Frank's cries. "Be sensible, man. Listen to me. I demand that you listen to me!"

CHAPTER TWENTY-FIVE

"NO, I'M QUITE SURE, thank you," I tell the taxi driver, as I hand him his fare. "I should like to walk the last stretch of the journey."

"Just like last time?" the driver says with a smile. "I remember you, Father. I brought you out this way a couple of months ago, didn't I?"

"You did," I reply, pleasantly surprised that I apparently made an impression on the gentleman. "Once again, let me express my gratitude for your good service. I wish you a pleasant day."

"It's getting late, though," he points out. "It'll be almost dark by the time you get to town."

"Nevertheless, I shall enjoy the stroll. Thank you for your concern."

As the driver sets off back in the other direction, I turn and start carrying my two suitcases along the road. I remember two months ago when I first arrived in Briarwych, I was filled with such optimism. Now, however, I must confess that the sight of the church spire ahead leaves me feeling rather apprehensive. I suppose I must simply put my head down and get to work, and hope that I can at least help *some* people from the local area.

Yet as I walk along the quiet road, somehow I feel I can still hear Frank Townley's maniacal laughter echoing in my thoughts.

***

Where is everybody?

As I make my way along the road that curves up toward the center of Briarwych, I cannot help but notice that I have so far seen not one soul. Granted, Briarwych is at best a quiet place, but there is usually evidence of some sort of activity. These evening, however, there are very few lights in any of the windows, and – as darkness begins to fall – I see none of the usual pre-blackout rush to get things done.

I tell myself that I should not be concerned, yet deep down I know that this is a very strange situation indeed.

By the time I get to the narrow main street, my worries have been compounded by the fact that the place is so very quiet. Up ahead, I can see lights in the window of the public house, but I hear none of the raucous merry-making that is the usual signature of that place. I might usually find all that palaver to be a sign of weak-willed low living, but right now I rather think I would be glad of *some* noise. And as I reach the public house and look through the window, I see that inside there are only a few lonesome individuals sitting around. Nursing their beers, they seem utterly sullen and completely uninterested in talking to one another.

I hesitate for a moment, knowing that I should simply keep going, but then I open the door to the public house and step inside. As I do so, the door's hinges creak loudly, immediately attracting attention from the few people gathered here inside. Faces turn and look at me, but they swiftly turn away again. Evidently the half-drunk pints of beer are of more interest.

"Good evening, gentlemen," I say, already feeling as if it was a mistake to come in here. "I trust that all is well."

The man at the nearest table grumbles something under his breath, but I do not catch the words and I do not – in the circumstances – feel that much would be gained by asking what he said.

"It's a fair evening out there," I continue, hoping to perhaps strike up a pleasant conversation with somebody. With *anybody*, really. "A little chilly when the breeze picks up, but otherwise quite fair indeed. Especially when one walks into town, and when one is able to marvel at the high tree-tops of the forest."

I wait.

Nobody says anything.

"Well, absolutely," I add finally. "Just an observation, that's all."

Again I wait.

Again, nobody even looks up at me.

I am about to turn and leave, when I see that Mr. Hendricks is one of the few souls in here. Sitting near the unlit fireplace, he is taking a sip of beer, so I make my way over to him. He is the closest thing to a friendly face right now.

"Good evening," I say. "Please, forgive the intrusion, but I cannot help but notice that -"

"There was an accident out at the airbase," he replies dourly.

I feel a flicker of fear in my chest.

"A young lad, only nineteen or so," he continues. "He wasn't part of the flying crews, as such. He worked on the ground, refueling and the like."

"What happened?" I ask.

"Something to do with the fuel catching light," he says. "He wasn't a lad from round here, he was shipped in to work on the base like most of the others, but people round here still take it hard when anything bad goes on. It was yesterday afternoon it took place, and since then nobody's felt much like getting on with things. It'll pass, but for now just let people be."

"I am so dreadfully sorry," I reply, as I set my suitcases down and take a seat. "Is the boy -"

"Last I heard is he was still hanging on," Hendricks continues, "but that was about lunchtime. From what they were saying about his injuries, I can't imagine it's still the case. Poor lad was covered from head to toe in flames, they said." At this, he makes the sign of the cross against his chest, and then he takes another sip of beer. "I'll tell you, Father. I can't get it out of my head. I keep imagining what it must have been like out there for him, even though I don't want to know. I prayed for him this afternoon, truly I did, but at times like this you start to wonder..."

He looks down at his hands, as if he's wondering what use a prayer can be in these troubled times.

"The Lord will look after the boy," I tell him.

"Will he?"

"Of course."

"Why couldn't he have looked after him before this happened?"

"He moves in -"

"Aye, I've heard that before. Mysterious ways."

At this, he rolls his eyes.

"But it's true," I continue. "The Lord has a plan for us all, and it is not always for us to know that plan until we reach his kingdom."

Hendricks opens his mouth, as if to argue with me, and for a moment I wait anxiously. Truth be told, I think I am at the limit of my calming words, and if challenged again I might have no answers. Fortunately, after a few seconds Hendricks takes another sip of beer and falls quiet, and I realize with a sense of relief that the moment has passed. He pauses, then he takes another sip, and then he glances at me again. Words seem, at least for now, to have failed him entirely, until suddenly he says something I had not been expecting:

"Can I buy you a pint, Father?"

"A pint?" I stare at him. "Of beer?"

"Well, you can have water if you really want, but I was thinking beer, yes."

"I..."

For a moment, I consider accepting this remarkable offer, if only to make a little connection with this man. Quickly, however, I realize that I can never do such a thing.

"It's okay," he says, as if he's anticipated my quandary, "I understand. Just a friendly suggestion, that's all. I thought you might want to actually get to know the people of Briarwych a little."

"I think I should go out to the airbase," I tell

him, "and see what I can do."

"I wouldn't bother until morning, Father. The lad'll be dead."

"But there will be others," I point out. "Men who witnessed what happened. I shall go and see what I can do."

He pauses, before nodding.

"That'd be mighty good of you, Father," he admits finally, before taking another sip of beer. "I'm sure there's some comfort you can offer them. Maybe you'll finally be useful round these parts."

***

Stepping into the church, I set my suitcases down and then go over to the office, from which I retrieve my bicycle. Already, night has begun to well and truly fall outside, but I know I simply *must* make the journey out to the airbase. As I turn my cycle toward the church's door, however, I am suddenly stopped by an overwhelming sense that I am not alone.

Standing in near-darkness, I turn and look along the corridor, and then I turn again and this time my gaze falls upon the distant altar. I know I should not indulge these foolish notions, especially so soon after listening to the mad ravings of that Francis Townley fellow in London, but for a few seconds I feel absolutely certain that there is somebody very close to me. I keep my eyes fixed upon the altar, convinced that at any moment I shall spot a hint of movement. A moment later, I hear a very faint, very distant rustling sound.

Or do I?

As soon as the sound has stopped, I am doubting it was ever there at all. I thought, just for a moment, that I heard the sound of fabric rustling, perhaps the creases of a skirt touching as a lady moved. There is quite clearly nobody here, yet this fear compels me to keep looking until finally I remind myself that time is of the essence.

Turning, I wheel my bicycle out of the church and then out of the gate, and then I mount the saddle and set off on the long, dark journey out to the RAF airbase. Lord knows what horror awaits me there.

CHAPTER TWENTY-SIX

"IT'S GOOD OF YOU to come out so late at night, Father," Corporal Bolton says as he leads me across the dark tarmac, toward the unlit building up ahead. "We'd heard you wouldn't be returning until tomorrow, or even the day after."

"I am so sorry that I was not here when the accident happened," I tell him. "I'm afraid I was in London, attending to some business."

"He was right, the poor lad," Bolton says, pushing the door open and turning to me. "He told us all you'd be back before he died."

"Before..."

I hesitate for a moment, as the meaning of those words sinks in.

"Do you mean to say," I continue finally, "that the victim is still alive?"

"If you can call it that," Bolton replies, with a hint of fear in his eyes. "He told us all he'd last until he got to speak to a priest. None of us believed him, but here you are. Looks like he was right all along." He pauses. "He was so certain, Father. So insistent. Quite remarkable, really, that he managed to cling to life for even this long."

I hesitate, before nodding. In truth, on my way out here I had assumed – after hearing what Mr. Hendricks had to say – that I would find a place of mourning. It did not really occur to me that the victim of this accident would still be on the base, yet now Bolton leads me inside and I spot the faint glow of candlelight coming from one of the rooms up ahead.

"The base's doctor wanted to move him to London," Bolton whispers, evidently keen not to be heard by the people in the next room, "but poor Charlie refused. The doctor figured he didn't have long left anyway, so he consented to let him remain here. It's surprised everyone how long he's managed to hang on, it's been more than twenty-four hours now, but he said he wanted to speak to a priest and, well, here you are."

I take a step forward, and now I realize that I can smell some kind of chemical mixture in the air, along with something that seems more organic. Is this, I cannot help but wonder, what burned human flesh smells like?

Suddenly two men appear from the room, silhouetted against the low candlelight.

"He wants to be alone with the priest," one of the men says. "That's who you are, isn't it?"

"It is," I reply. "I mean... I am, yes."

"I need to get outside for a moment," the other man says, slipping past me. "I need some fresh air. And some beer."

"Me too."

"We'll be outside, Father," Bolton adds. "The other boys are in the mess hall, or asleep. Everybody's just waiting for..."

His voice trails off, and then he heads out with the other two, leaving me alone in the hallway. A moment later I hear a faint groan from the next room, and I realize that I cannot delay. I step forward to the doorway, and then I look through and see that although the room is lit only by the light of a solitary candle, I can just about make out the shape of a man on a bed pushed against the far wall. Nearby, a trolley contains various syringes and bottles, probably left behind by the doctor after pain medication was administered.

The smell in the room is intense, thick with ammonia and bleach and other aromas that I cannot quite place.

Suddenly the figure on the bed lets out a harsher, more anguished gasp, as if my presence has been noted.

"I am here, my child," I say, stepping into the room and approaching the side of the bed. I must put aside all my aversions, and I must comfort this poor, dying man. "It is Father Loveford, from Briarwych."

The figure groans again. In the low light, I can make out barely much more than his outline, although in truth I am a little relieved that I cannot see the full extent of his injuries. Even now, I can just about see that the skin on his hands is horribly burned, with bloodied and discolored patches, and I cannot help but feel shocked that such a badly-hurt man could even be alive in such a state. His pain and suffering must be incredible, and I truly cannot understand how he could have survived this long.

And then I see that he is holding a small white cross.

Barely half as long as one of his fingers, the cross is so simple and so plain. It is completely white, save for smears of blood and other bodily fluids that have been trailed along all its sides. After a moment, the man's fingers turn the cross around a little, and it's quite clear to me in this instant that the poor fellow is deriving a great deal of comfort from this simple symbol of his faith.

"I thought I might perhaps read to you," I tell him, as I take the Bible from my pocket. For some reason, my hands are trembling a little. "If there are any passages that you particularly -"

Before I can finish, he lets out another gasp, louder than before and more pained.

Startled, I look at the man and see the silhouette of his face, and the light from the candle picks out the very edge of his horrific burns. This poor soul barely looks human anymore, and I quickly glance down at the Bible so that I do not have to see such injuries. God forgive me for such cowardice, but I simply cannot observe such obvious, terrible pain.

"I can choose some passages," I continue, even as I feel utterly useless. "There are certainly some that might comfort you, in this time of -"

Suddenly he gasps again, and this time he tilts his head back. I stare at him for a moment, not knowing what to do but fighting the impulse to simply flee the room and call for the doctor. Ordinarily I would reach out and hold the fellow's hand, but in this situation I worry that I might inadvertently cause him a great deal of pain. I have only words, then, so I suppose I must search the Bible for some suitable passages. Before I can do so, however, the man tilts his head back even further and opens his mouth wide, and a faint clicking sound seems to be coming from the back of his throat.

He is trying to say something.

"What is it, my child?" I ask. "Tell me."

The sound continues, but I cannot pick out

any words.

"You must not trouble yourself too greatly," I explain. "Please, allow me to read to you, and then -"

Suddenly his whole body shudders, and he lets out a long sigh. I freeze, staring at him, and then as the seconds tick past I realize that not only is he no longer moving, but that I do not hear any indication that he is breathing. I watch intently, holding my own breath even, but the man has now fallen entirely still, and I am beginning to fear that he has perhaps reached his end. Indeed, as the second tick silently past, I come to realize that this is truly the case. I arrived in time to see the poor man, but too late to read to him or to provide any real comfort.

He is dead.

Finally, realizing that there is nothing else left for me to do, I read a few passages from the Bible out loud, and I pray for the man's soul, and then I get to my feet and head out of the room.

"Is it over?" Bolton asks.

"It is," I reply.

"We expected as much," he says, as the two other men slip silently into the room. "We felt he was hanging on for a priest to come. He was a great believer in all of that, Father. We all say we are here, but Charlie used to pray morning, noon and night. He was a good lad. What happened to him was a tragedy, but at least he's not suffering now."

"Amen," I whisper.

I pause for a moment, unsure as to what I might say yet still certain that I should say *something*. After all, it is my role to bring comfort to those who are suffering.

"I am sure," I manage finally, "that I was not the only reason he hung on for so long."

"And I'm sure you were," he replies. "Or do you not think faith is that strong, Father?"

"Of course it is, but..."

My voice trails off. Is it really possible that that poor, injured boy managed to cling to life just so that he could see a priest before he died?

"Thank you for coming out," Bolton continues. "I know it might not feel as if you did much, but I'm sure you gave him great comfort. If nothing else, your sitting with him for a few minutes gave him the peace he needed in order to let go. He'll be sent home for burial, of course. There's a family out there who'll have to be informed."

"Of course," I tell him. "If there is anything I can do to help, you must let me know."

"I just wish I understood what had caused the accident," he continues. "He was always so careful, he used to remind the others about the safety procedures. I can't believe he'd have cut corners like this, in a way that could lead to something terrible happening."

"We all make mistakes," I point out.

"Not Charlie," he replies, as he looks back through into the room, toward the dead body. "Charlie was one of my best workers. Something must have caused him to make a mistake. There's something we're not seeing here."

CHAPTER TWENTY-SEVEN

BY THE TIME I get back to the church, midnight has well and truly passed. I must confess that, as I push my bicycle through the doorway, I feel utterly exhausted. This is hardly surprising, given that I traveled today first from London to Briarwych by train, and then by bicycle out to the airbase and back. Still, I have to be up bright and early tomorrow morning, to resume my duties and to arrange for the poor dead man's burial.

After shutting the door, I lean my bicycle against the wall and then I start making my way toward the kitchen, only to suddenly stop and look through toward the distant altar.

I am not alone.

I feel the sensation more strongly than ever now. There is somebody here with me in the church, somebody unseen, and I believe I just heard another faint rustle of fabric. Earlier I was able to deceive myself into thinking that this was nonsense, but now the belief is getting stronger and stronger and finally I walk over to the back row of pews and stop again, listening for any hint of a presence.

Finally, I am unable to keep myself from speaking.

"Hello?" I call out, my voice echoing slightly in the cold darkness of the church. "Is anybody there?"

I wait.

Silence.

This is ludicrous. I am allowing recent events to get the better of me, so I turn to go to the kitchen, only to suddenly hear a very faint but very definite bumping sound coming from somewhere near the altar.

I turn again, but now the sound has stopped.

"Hello?" I say cautiously, struck by the sound of fear in my own voice. "Is... I mean, are there... I mean, is anybody here? If there is somebody, I would like you to show yourself immediately."

Again, there is no reply.

I want to simply go to the kitchen, to put this all down to a moment of exhausted fear, but instead I force myself to start walking along the aisle, heading toward the altar. I know that I shall find nothing there, of course, but I cannot help glancing around in case there is any sign of another figure here in the church with me. One can try to be as stoic and as logical as one likes in these moments, but there are times when we all let our defenses down. And as I reach the altar, I take a deep breath and -

Suddenly I freeze as I see her.

A woman is kneeling on the stone floor just a few feet away, with her head bowed and her hands clasped together. For a fraction of a second I am seized by fear, gripped by the belief that this must be the terrible sight of Judith Prendergast herself, but then as I take a step back I realize that there is something familiar about both the white dress that the figure is wearing and about the curve of the back and the curls of the hair that hangs down to cover the side of her face.

"Lizzy?" I whisper, as I realize that it is indeed she. "Are you quite alright?"

I wait, but she does not respond. She does not do anything to even indicate that she is aware of my presence.

"Lizzy," I say again, taking a step closer. "It's me, Father Loveford. I have returned a little early. What are you doing here so late?"

Still, she does not respond, although she shifts slightly and I hear that same rustling of fabric that I first heard earlier before I went out to the airbase. She must have been here all that time, if not longer, and now it's almost as if she is in some kind of trance. She simply remains kneeling in the moonlight.

"Lizzy, it is late," I say, stepping even closer and then reaching down and touching her shoulder. Instantly, I am shocked by how ice-cold the shoulder feels through the thin fabric of her dress.

I wait.

Why does she not look at me?

"Lizzy," I continue, trying to sound a little more authoritative, "I really must insist that you get to your feet. I'm sorry, but I am very tired and I do not think I am in a fit state to offer any help at this time. Unless something specific has happened, I must ask that you rise. You shouldn't even be in here this late, I only left a key with you because I wanted you to be able to clean while I was gone. You were not supposed to let yourself in like this."

I wait.

Nothing.

"Lizzy!"

I pull on her shoulder.

Suddenly she gasps and pulls back, slumping against the edge of a nearby pew. At the same moment, she looks up at me with a wide-open mouth, and in the moonlight I am shocked to see that her eyes are completely white.

Startled, I step back.

Whimpering as if she is in terrible distress, Lizzy rolls onto her side and puts her arms across her face, almost as if she is momentarily blinded by a great light. Her whole body convulses and then, just as I am trying to work out what I should do next, she lowers her arms and rolls onto her back, and she looks up at me with eyes that are – blessedly – slowly returning to their normal state. They must have been rolled far back in their sockets.

She says nothing as she stares at me, and it is almost as if she does not recognize me at all.

"Lizzy," I manage to say finally, "what in the name of all that's holy is going on here? Are you quite alright?"

I wait for her to explain herself, but she continues to simply stare up at me. In the moonlight, her face looks quite pale indeed, almost sickly.

"Lizzy..."

"I'm sorry!" she stammers, suddenly starting to get to her feet.

I take hold of her arm to help her, but then she bumps against me and attempts to push past. Still unable to determine what is happening, I keep hold of her tight, forcing her to remain.

She struggles again, before slipping and falling hard against the edge of one of the pews.

"Careful!" I tell her. "You'll do yourself

damage!"

"I'm sorry!" she says again, sounding now as if she is on the verge of bursting into tears as she scrambles to her feet. "Please, I'm so sorry!"

"You keep saying that," I reply, "but whatever is the matter? This is most unlike you, Lizzy. What are you doing here so late?"

She turns to me, and then she looks at the altar. I can see from the expression on her face that she is entirely lost. She glances around, as if she is looking for somebody else, and truly she looks to have taken leave of her senses.

"I don't know what happened," she says finally, her voice trembling with fear. "I came earlier, to do some additional cleaning, and the whole church was so still and peaceful, and then..."

She hesitates, and now there are tears in her eyes as she turns to me.

"I don't remember," she whimpers, as the first tears start rolling down her cheeks. "Father Loveford, I am so sorry, but I don't remember a thing! I came to clean, but that must have been hours ago. It was daylight and everything seemed absolutely fine, and then suddenly I find that I am here and it's night and I don't understand what can have happened!"

I stare at her, watching her eyes for any hint of that utter whiteness that I saw just a moment ago.

"My eyes hurt," she whispers, as if she

herself is in a state of shock. Reaching up, she touches her lower eyelids. "They're sore."

She hesitates for a moment, before turning to me.

"What?" she asks. "Why are you looking at me like that? What's wrong?"

"Nothing's wrong," I reply, choosing to keep from upsetting her further. There is no need to tell her what I think I saw, especially since it was most likely a trick of the light.

"Oh, Father Loveford!" she sobs, suddenly stepping toward me and putting her arms around me, holding me tight. "It's so frightful that I don't know what happened. You must think that I have entirely lost my mind!"

"Of course not," I reply, although I must confess that this possibility had begun to occur to me. "It is late, and you are tired. You are not the only one. Most likely, this will all make a great deal more sense in the light of morning. Why, I often find that a good night's sleep is all that's needed for one to come to one's senses. I myself am greatly tired, and in truth I barely feel as if I can function. Let us talk more in the morning."

I wait, but she continues to sob, and finally I put my arms around her. This feels rather forward of me, yet I know that I must offer the poor girl some comfort. There is also the fact that, deep down, I like the closeness, and for a moment I breathe deep the simple smell of her hair. I believe I would very much like to continue holding Lizzy, and that in turn she would benefit from my -

"No," I say suddenly, pulling away as I realize that this is wrong. "I'm sorry, but we shall have to continue this in the morning."

"But Father -"

"I need to sleep," I add, surprised by my own weakness. "Lizzy, please, you too need to get some rest. You are not due to clean tomorrow, but please come anyway if you feel the need to do so. Or don't. It's entirely up to you. But for tonight, I must retire to bed. Alone."

I feel rather callous, but at the same time I worry about what might happen were Lizzy to stay. I very much value my restraint, yet something about Lizzy makes me doubt whether I could hold back. I might do something that I would later regret very much.

Lizzy pauses, as if she might be about to remonstrate with me, but then she takes a step back.

"Of course, Father," she says, furrowing her brow for a moment, and then she turns and hurries along the aisle as if she cannot wait to get out of here. Perhaps she sensed the same informality that has left me a little flustered.

"I shall be here in the morning!" I call out, worried that perhaps I was a little too short with her, that I drove her away. "Feel free to come and speak to me, if you wish. Lizzy? I shall be here in the -"

Before I can finish, I hear the door slam shut, and I let out a sigh as I realize that perhaps I could have handled that situation a little better. Then again, I cannot afford to let the girl get too close to me, since she might start to get the wrong idea. She is young and impressionable, and I would estimate that there are perhaps twelve years between our two ages, perhaps even as many as fifteen. That, I feel, is a little too large a gap for a man to consider a potential wife. After all, social norms must be observed.

It is for the best that I sent her away.

Taking a deep breath, I look around one final time before making my way back along the aisle. I must put all thoughts of Lizzy out of my mind for tonight. At the same time, I cannot help thinking back to the sight of her eyes rolled back in their sockets. Something about Lizzy looked most unusual tonight. Almost unreal.

CHAPTER TWENTY-EIGHT

BRIGHT MORNING LIGHT STREAMS through the stained-glass windows, as I step out of my office and walk over to collect my bike. After a good night's sleep, I am ready to get on with the tasks of the day. Indeed, I feel rather refreshed and energized.

As I reach the door, however, I see that a note has been slipped under the gap.

Reaching down, I pick the note up and unfold it, and I immediately recognize Lizzy's writing. Somehow, deep down, I already know that this note will surely not contain good news:

Dear Father Loveford,

I am afraid I must go away for a while.

I am so sorry to leave under these circumstances, and I can only hope that you will be able to find another cleaner. I do not know when I shall return, so it might be for the best if you engage somebody else on a permanent basis.

I am sorry for troubling you last night, and I wish you all the best with your future work at the church. I am certain that soon you shall have full attendance, and that you will be extremely successful here in Briarwych. I have the utmost faith in your abilities. I wish you all the best, and again I offer my profuse apologies.

Yours,

Lizzy

I read the note through for a second time, hoping that I have misunderstood, but once I get back to the end I realize with a heavy heart that this is indeed a goodbye. Stepping outside, I look around, just in case there is any chance that I might yet spot her leaving, but all I see is the beautiful, sun-dappled grass and the gravestones that are all around in the cemetery.

Lizzy must have left this note some time ago, before I rose even. Now, it seems, she is gone from Briarwych. And somehow that thought leaves the beauty of the world a little dimmed.

***

"You won't have any luck there," a voice says, just as I am about to knock for a third time on the cottage's door. "There's nobody in."

Turning, I see that a lady has emerged from the house next door. She's not somebody I've seen before, but she has that same expression of disdain that I have – unfortunately – encountered so many times already during my time here in Briarwych.

"I saw her leaving this morning," she continues, folding her arms as she leans against the jamb. "Didn't take much with her, but then I don't know that she had much to begin with. I asked where she was going, but she was sobbing. Then she just went off down the road, and that's the last of her." She sniffs. "Hopefully, anyway. I was wondering for a while when she might be on her way."

"Does she have any family in the area?" I ask, shocked by this news.

"Are you serious?"

"She must have someone," I continue. "I'm

terribly sorry, I know this might seem rather foolish of me, but I would like to check and make sure that she's alright. Does she, perhaps, have friends or relations in a nearby town?"

"I'd leave her alone, if I were you. Join the rest of us in hoping she doesn't come back."

"I think that's rather unnecessary," I point out, as the lady turns to go back into her home. "Lizzy is a fine young lady and I for one have found her assistance to be invaluable."

"People don't want her around here," she replies, glancing back at me. "Why would they? Why would anyone in Briarwych want the daughter of Judith Prendergast still knocking about, reminding them of what happened."

"The daughter of..."

My voice trails off as I try to make sense of what the lady just said.

"You did know, didn't you?" she continues, and then a hint of a smile reaches her face. "Oh, bless you, tell me you knew, Father. How could you not?"

I swallow hard.

"Did she not tell you?" she asks, and now she's not even trying to hide her amusement. "Oh, my Tom'll love it when I tell him. Everyone will. Why do you think no-one wanted to come to your services, Father? As far as people in Briarwych are concerned, we don't want any reminders of that horrible woman."

"Lizzy is Miss Prendergast's daughter?" I reply. "Are you sure?"

She rolls her eyes.

"That's the irony, isn't it?" she points out. "Judith Prendergast claimed to be a woman of great virtue, but she had a child out of wedlock. With a boy from another village, they say. If you believe the stories, that's what made her so holier-than-thou. Those people are always hypocrites in the end, aren't they?"

"But how could that be?" I continue. "It would have come up in conversation, unless..."

My voice trails off as I realize the truth.

Lizzy's parentage would indeed have come up in conversation, unless she had made a deliberate effort to conceal this fact from me.

"We're all best shot of her," the woman says, in a very matter-of-fact tone, as if the matter is settled. "The only pity's that it took her this long to realize she's not welcome. Her father died some time back, her mother's dead too now. There's nothing and no-one for her in Briarwych, not anymore. She's not wanted."

With that, she heads inside and shuts her door, leaving me standing in a state of shock in the road. There is a part of me that finds this news impossible to believe, and that wonders why Lizzy would not have mentioned something so important;

after all, this revelation means that Lizzy actually saw her own mother's body being removed from the church. I don't want to believe that she would have kept something like this from me, yet at the same time there was always something rather furtive about Lizzy, a kind of nervous energy that I could never quite explain.

As I turn and start making my way back toward the church, I rack my brains in an attempt to work out whether there were any clues that I missed. I pride myself on being a rather intuitive man, yet the truth about Lizzy eluded me entirely. I try to think of any moments when I could have missed the obvious. All the time, however, it is becoming increasingly clear that Lizzy sought to hide the truth, and that she must simply have been lucky that I did not learn her true identity from any other source. Now that I think back, I realize that she quite often avoided being with me when anybody else came to the church, with the exception of a few services.

Still, though, I cannot believe that the truth did not emerge before now. Or that Lizzy would actively try to deceive me.

"She used to work for Father Perkins," I remember Lizzy saying once, when the subject of Judith Prendergast came up. "Nobody like her. Oh, I probably shouldn't say that, but it's true. She was shrill and vicious. Even Father Perkins abhorred her, although he was far too well-mannered to say as much. In truth, I believe they're right when they say that by the end she was mad, quite out of her mind. I mean, I suppose that's why, in the end, when he locked her inside, nobody wanted to come and let her out. Not at first. I was younger then, of course, but I heard people saying that she could stew in there for a while."

She was so clear about the matter, she showed no hint of excess emotion. Yet all the time, she was talking about her own mother. What must the poor girl have been going through? What awful pain must have been tearing at her heart? I want to find her, to talk to her, to learn what she was really thinking and why she chose to spend so much time at the place where her mother died.

But I can't, because now she is gone.

CHAPTER TWENTY-NINE

One month later

"I'M SO SORRY TO have disturbed you, Father,"
Mrs. Neill says tearfully as she leads me up the
stairs in her home, "but he's so much worse than he
was before. I know you're not a doctor, but if you
could just pray for him..."

"Of course," I reply, stopping at the top of
the stairs as I realize that I can smell sickness in the
air. There is something so very sweet about that
aroma usually, and I always find that the sweeter
the smell, the closer the victim is to death. In this
instance, the sweetness is overpowering. "Anything
I can do to help."

And yet I hesitate for a moment, since the
boy sounds so terribly ill. Curiously, I have always

found children the most difficult to deal with in such circumstances. When an adult is sick, one can simply commend the sufferer's soul to the Lord; with a child, I can never shake the niggling feeling that somehow this is not right, that the Lord should protect all those who are young.

Mrs. Neill disappears into the room, and a moment later I hear her talking in hushed tones with her husband.

Taking a deep breath, I step forward.

And then, suddenly, I hear the most dreadful sobbing sound coming from the room. A fraction of a second later, Mrs. Neill rushes out and hurries into another room, and then her husband appears in the doorway that leads to the child. As soon as I see his face, I know what must have happened.

"He passed away," he says, his voice tense with the effort of holding back tears. "Little Jack, I mean. He breathed his last while his mother was out fetching you." He sighs. "She'll blame herself for that, she will. For not being with him when it happened, I mean. I know my wife, and I'm telling you, she'll think she let him down."

"I am so sorry," I reply.

He pauses, before nodding.

In the next room, Mrs. Neill is weeping loudly. More than weeping, actually; the sound is primal, like something one might expect to hear from a distressed animal. It is pure grief.

"I must go to her," Mr. Neill says.

"Might I sit with young Jack for a moment?" I ask.

"Is there any point now, Father?"

"I should like to. Very much."

He pauses, before nodding, and then he goes into the other room. Left alone on the landing for a moment, I take a deep breath, and then I walk into the next room, where I stop as soon as I see the dead little boy on his bed. His eyes are closed and his mouth is slightly open, but otherwise death is so recent that he looks remarkably healthy. A little pale, perhaps, but one could almost believe that he might open his eyes at any moment.

Almost.

I step over to the bed, before taking a seat. Every movement, every sound, feels like an intrusion in a room where it seems that silence should reign. Even as I hear Mrs. Neill still weeping in the next room, I feel that I should not make any noise at all. Even a prayer might be too loud, no matter how quietly whispered. Instead, then, I look over at the face of the dead boy, as his mother's muffled sobs continue in the next room.

At some point, somebody is bound to ask me why a young boy should die. Why God would let this happen.

And I shall say...

Before I can finish that thought, I hear a

creaking sound out on the landing. I glance at the empty doorway without thinking, and in an instant I realize that somebody is out there. I had thought that Mr. Neill and his wife were in the other bedroom and that nobody else was here in the house, but the sound seemed rather close. I wait, but the sound does not return, and finally I look down at my hands.

The smell of death is sweeter than ever.

"Why does God let children die?" somebody will doubtless ask me. "Why did poor Jack have to suffer?"

I have been asked many questions over the years, and I have always had an answer to give. When the matter turns to children, however, I feel a hollowness where I should instead feel certainty. I feel doubt, where I should feel faith. For I do not know why the Lord lets children suffer in this manner, and I have never found an answer that can satisfy either the asker or myself.

I need the Lord's guidance.

I need to know why -

Suddenly the creaking sound returns. I look over at the doorway, and but there is nobody there so I look back down at my hands.

"Lord," I whisper, "give me the strength to comfort these people. Show me the way forward, so that I might in turn guide these poor souls who have lost their son."

I pause, trying to think of the right words.

Nothing comes.

"Give me the strength to guide these lost souls," I whisper, even though I know I am repeating myself, "and to... strengthen their faith, and to guide their souls and -"

Suddenly I hear the creak again. I look up, exasperated, and then I am about to look back at my hands when I freeze.

A young boy is standing in the doorway, watching me.

I could lie. I could pretend that it is not young Jack, that the dead boy beside me is not now also standing before me, but to what avail? Already I know deep down that it is him, as he turns and looks at me with dead, mournful eyes. There is something accusatory in his gaze, as if he blames me, and he continues to stare at me for a moment longer before finally turning and walking out of view. I hear the creak of another floorboard, and then I realize that he must have gone into the room where his father is consoling his mother.

I wait, certain that I shall hear a scream, but in fact I hear nothing.

Finally I turn and look at Jack's body. His face remains as before – with closed eyes and a mouth that hangs slightly open – but otherwise he looks exactly as he looked a moment ago in the doorway.

It was him.

No.

No, it cannot have been him.

I get to my feet, still clutching my Bible. I had planned to sit here for a while longer, but now my chest is filled with something approximating panic. I make my way to the door and then out onto the landing, and then I hesitate for a moment outside the door to the other bedroom. I can still hear Mrs. Neill weeping, and occasionally her husband offers some hushed comfort, but other than that I hear no other sounds coming from the room, and certainly nothing to suggest that little Jack is in there. The door, however, is slightly ajar, so I step closer and wait a moment longer, and then I knock gently.

"Come in," I hear Mr. Neill say.

I hesitate again, and then I push the door open.

"Thank you, Father," Mr. Neill continues, sitting on the bed with an arm around his wife, while the figure of little Jack stands just a little further along. "As I'm sure you'll appreciate, my wife is still very upset. Even though we knew this was coming, we..."

His voice trails off.

I cannot avert my gaze from Jack, who stands – apparently unnoticed by his parents – next to the far end of the bed. A single candle is burning, casting flickering shadows on the side of his face as he stares back at me. His expression is calm and firm, almost as if he is challenging me to say something about his presence.

"He was our only child, you know," Mr. Neill continues, his voice starting to break slightly. "We thought he'd grow up to be such a good man. He was smart, smarter than he had any right to be, coming from us. But he *was* smart and he had such a bright future ahead. Now he's gone and..."

Again, his voice fades to nothing.

I continue to stare at Jack, still not quite able to believe that he is here.

"I suppose," Mr. Neill adds, "that we shall have to start thinking about a ceremony. If it's alright with you, though, can we talk about that tomorrow? As strange as it might sound, we'd like to have Jack with us here for one more night. Please don't judge us for that, it's just that we'd like one more night with him in his room, even if... Well, I'm sure you can understand. He can go in the morning, can't he?"

"He..."

I stare at Jack for a moment longer, before finally forcing myself to look at his father.

"We can talk in the morning, yes," I stammer, as a cold shiver passes through my chest. "Take your time."

"It's cold in here," Mrs. Neill says suddenly,

pulling away from her husband and heading over to the already-closed window, where she proceeds to check that the latches are properly in place. There are tears in her eyes as she turns first to her husband, and then to me. "Isn't it?" she continues, as another tear rolls down her face. "It's not just me, it *is* cold in here."

I look down at Jack, who continues to stare at me. Is that scorn I see in his eyes? Perhaps he simply wants me to leave, so that he can be alone with his grieving parents. Either that, or he sees my inability to help, and he knows that I am full of nothing more than empty answers.

"I should go," I say suddenly, turning and stepping out onto the landing, and I feel instantly relieved now that I can no longer see the face of the dead child. "I can see myself out."

I hesitate for a moment, steadying myself against the top of the banister, trying to calm my nerves. I feel utterly shaken and completely useless, as if all my claims to faith have been stripped away.

Finally, choked by the sweet smell of death in the house, and filled with a sense of dread, I realize that I have to get out of here.

On the verge of panic, I hurry down the stairs. Mrs. Neil was right to say that the bedroom was cold, yet at the same time the house suddenly feels dreadfully stuffy and airless, and as I get outside into the night air I feel rather breathless. I am able to instantly recover, however, as soon as I am outside, and I stop to take in some big gulps of air, before turning and reaching out to take hold of the door handle.

For a moment, I listen to the sound of Mrs. Neill's continued sobs, and then I very gently pull the front door shut and step back to look up at the cottage's upper windows. The blackout curtains are in place, of course, so the light from the candle is blocked. I know that they are in there, however, and I cannot help but think of the sight of Jack sitting on the bed next to his parents. He looked so real, as if he was really present in death.

Yet I know that he cannot have been.

In fact, with each step back that I take from the cottage, I feel my concerns fade further away. The atmosphere in that bedroom must have been so utterly oppressive that I allowed my thoughts to run wild. May the Lord have mercy, for I weakened and saw a most unholy vision. Now I must forget that vision and be strong, for a crack in the mind can easily grow to become a chasm, and one must be forever on-guard. I had a momentary blip, that's all. A small wobble.

Ghosts are not real. They are simply not part of the Lord's plan.

CHAPTER THIRTY

ONE WEEK LATER, I perform my first funeral service here at Briarwych.

A small crowd attends. Jack and his parents have long been popular in the village, it seems, and news of the boy's death has brought a few to the cemetery who I have not seen here previously. By the time the coffin is lowered into the ground, there are almost a dozen people gathered around the grave, while Mr. and Mrs. Neill stand at the far end as their son's body is committed to the ground. I have already spoken now, although I know that no words can counter the terrible grief that the Neills and the wider community must be feeling. Yet as I conclude the ceremony, it is clear that nobody else here has noticed the young boy who stands a little way back from the grave.

Little Jack has come to his own funeral.

I have so far managed to avoid looking directly at the child, for fear of encouraging what must surely be some kind of apparition. Yet out of the corner of my eye I still see the boy, and in truth I feel a glimmer of relief as I tell the mourners that the service is over. I step back and allow those gathered to talk amongst themselves, and then I make my way around to speak directly to the mourning parents. When I offer to take them into the church and discuss matters with them privately, I am surprised by their willingness, so I lead them toward the door.

Glancing over my shoulder, I feel a stir of dread as I see that Jack is following us. Not rushing, not attempting to attract our attention in any way; he is simply keeping pace with us, a few steps behind.

"It was a beautiful ceremony," Mrs. Neill says, as she sniffs back tears. "Your words gave me some comfort, Father, and I did not think that was possible."

"It'll take time," her husband replies. "We'll get through it together. And when Anthony gets back from the war, he'll move in with us and train to take over the shop."

"We don't know that he'll -"

"Of course he'll be coming back," Mr. Neill adds, interrupting her. "The war can't last forever, you know. And he's a smart lad. He's clever. He'll keep himself out of trouble."

"My door is always open," I tell them, leading them into the church and then toward the office.

Reaching the doorway, I turn and look back at them. To my surprise, I see that although Mr. and Mrs. Neill have both followed me inside, young Jack has stopped at the main door and is staring along the corridor with an expression of fear. For the first time he is looking not at me, but at something at the corridor's far end that seems to have caught his attention. I turn and follow his gaze, but all I see is empty stone walls and a couple of doors leading off into other parts of the church.

Turning once more to Jack, I see that he has now taken a step back, and that the expression on his face seems to be slowly turning into one of fear. It is as if something in the church is scaring him.

"Father?"

Startled, I turn and see that the Neill's are staring at me. After a moment Mr. Neill looks over his shoulder, straight toward the spot where Jack is still backing away from the church's threshold, but then he turns to me again as if he saw nothing out of the ordinary.

"Are you alright?" he asks.

"Of course," I reply, before looking again along the corridor toward the empty spot that seems to so terrify young Jack. "I merely -"

For a moment, I spot a shadow moving against the far wall, a faint darkening of the stones that seems to fall in the shape of a passing woman. And then, in an instant, that shadow is gone. I watch, waiting for the cause to become apparent, but now the shadows is completely absent. It must, I suppose, have been some trick of the light, perhaps something that showed through one of the windows.

I turn to the Neills.

"I'm sorry," I continue, "I only -"

Before I can finish, I hear footsteps nearby, and I turn just in time to see Corporal Bolton hurrying into the church.

"I want a word with you, Father Loveford," he says firmly, giving the impression that he's rather angry about something. "Now!"

***

"A spy?" I say, shocked by the suggestion. "Whatever are you talking about, why in the name of all that's holy would you think *I* might be harboring a spy?"

"I know your lot," he replies, still eyeing me with a hint of suspicion. "You think all souls are worthy of being saved, all that nonsense. You probably think Jerry's not bad, underneath it all, and that they're all just following orders."

"I assure you, I -"

"I need you to promise me, Father," he continues, "that you know absolutely nothing about a German spy who might be in the area. That you haven't heard so much as a whisper!"

"I know nothing!" I tell him, unable to hide the fact that I feel rather insulted by the suggestion. "How can you even think such a thing? I am a patriotic Englishman and I am doing my bit for the war."

Sighing, he heads over to the window and looks out for a moment, and then he turns to me again.

"I would be out there myself," I explain, unable to hide a hint of indignation, "were it not for my damaged leg. Do you think I didn't try to sign up? I went to three separate centers and tried to conceal my disability, but I was turned away each time. I am a man of the cloth, yes, but don't you dare think for one moment that I chose not to be out there with our brave soldiers!"

I pause for a moment, and I already feel that I perhaps allowed myself to get too easily riled.

"I did not mean that to come out the way that it did," I add. "I merely... I won't be accused of being soft when it comes to the war. And I assure you, I would be the first to turn in any spy in this vicinity."

"I'm sorry, Father," he says with a sigh. "I

suppose I'm letting it get to me, but our airbase is one of the most important in the country. We already know that Jerry's onto our existence, but we're safe so long as our precise location remains hidden. If there's a Jerry spy in the area, the entire project could be jeopardized. I can't tell you the details of the planes we're developing, or the payloads, but they could be enough to bring this bloody war to an end."

"And what exactly makes you think that there might be a spy nearby?" I ask.

"First it was those petrol cans that went missing," he explains. "Let's just say that they're an experimental mixture."

"So they were mislaid."

"We have procedures in place to ensure that experimental items aren't mislaid."

"Procedures fail sometimes."

"Not my procedures, Father."

"That doesn't mean that a spy's involved."

"Then there's the tent," he continues. "Two of my men were taking a shortcut back to the base through the forest, and they discovered a tent out there in the middle of nowhere, about five miles from the base. It's obvious someone's been living there for a while."

"And was there anything in the tent to suggest that Germans are involved?"

"No, but -"

"So perhaps it's just a vagrant," I suggest, "or a draft-dodger. There are plenty of possible explanations."

"And I'm supposed to accept that it's just a coincidence that they're near the airbase?"

"Coincidences *do* happen," I remind him.

"It just seems to be too much," he says with another sigh. "We've seen an increase in the number of German bombers that fly within fifty miles of the base. It looks like they're starting to narrow down our location. If they manage to hit us, Loveford, they could set the war effort back by six months. We thought about moving some of the most sensitive test programs, but that'd pretty much set us back by the same amount of time. I'm sorry, Father, I didn't mean to come storming in here and start accusing you of treason, but..."

I wait, but he seems to be at his wits end.

"What did you find in the tent?" I ask, hoping to be helpful.

"Not a lot. Some rations, some clothes."

"And nobody has been back to claim any of this?"

"I've had two men stationed out there, keeping an eye on the place. If the bugger knows his hiding place has been rumbled, there's no way he'd return. I've got to be honest, Loveford. My men are jumpy as hell. They'll shoot on sight if they so much as see a leaf blowing through that forest at the moment."

"Let us hope that no accidents occur due to this," I suggest.

"Something's going on," he continues, still looking out the window as if he hopes the answer might suddenly appear. "Something I can't see, even though I know it's there. And that's driving me mad, Father. I need answers, or I think I'm liable to go stir bloody crazy."

I look along to the far end of the corridor, but now there are no shifting shadows and I am quickly able to convince myself that I have merely – of late – allowed my imagination to run a little wild. At the same time, I feel the I understand Corporal Bolton's predicament all too well. Here too in the church there seems to be something going on, something just beyond my understanding. I need to understand what this 'something' is, before my imagination starts running wild.

First, however, I need to confront the fact that even a child's funeral was not enough to draw more than a few mourners to the church. It is time, I believe, for the people of this village to face facts.

CHAPTER THIRTY-ONE

"IS THIS HOW YOU choose to mark the passing of a child?"

As soon as those words leave my lips, the laughter stops and the denizens of the public house turn to me. Perhaps I raised my voice a little too much, but I'm afraid that I am at my wit's end with these people, and I feel not an ounce of regret as I step forward and look around at the faces that, in turn, stare back at me with expressions ranging from shock to incredulity and even amusement.

"A child was laid to rest today," I continue, with my voice trembling slightly, "and where were you all?"

I wait, but not one of these miscreants dares answer me. They simply sit, staring, some even with their mugs of beer still in their hands and waiting to be sipped.

"You all knew little Jack Neill, I assume," I say, stepping into the middle of the saloon and looking round once again. "You must certainly know his parents. Good people, they are, and fine upstanding members of this village. Yet not one of you -"

"Father -"

"I am speaking!" I roar, turning to the man who dared try to interrupt me.

He stares, clearly shocked by my outburst.

"Not one of you came to show your support today," I continue. "In this time of need, not one of you gave even one ounce of your compassion or pity. And why not, eh? What is it that kept you away from the church?"

Another man opens his mouth to speak.

"Guilt!" I say firmly.

The man hesitates, before closing his mouth.

"It's guilt you all feel, is it not?" I ask. "These months, I have been opening the doors of the church, I have been running services, and barely anybody has bothered to show up. And it's because of a sense of guilt. I see that now. When Judith Prendergast got locked inside the church, nobody bothered to check up on her. Maybe you laughed, or maybe you simply scared yourselves witless with childish ghost stories, but the upshot is that a woman died and rotted in that place and not one of you went to check on her."

I look around at some more of the men, and now it is as if one could hear a pin drop in the silence.

"Basic human care," I continue. "That's what you all lacked. And now, rather than face up to what you did, or rather to what you didn't do, you sit here and drink yourselves silly. You choose to forget, rather than to face up, to your sins. Even if that means foregoing service on a Sunday, or if it means neglecting to attend the funeral of a child. You'll do anything to avoid facing up to your collective guilt."

"Would you care for an ale, Father?" the barman asks.

I turn and glare at him.

"Just a little joke," he adds.

"You can all be forgiven at the church," I say, turning to some of the other men and spotting Hendricks among them. "Not here, not in this den of iniquity. You'll find nothing here but more misery, for all this ale will not change anything, it will only exaggerate what you already feel. The guilt, the shame... All shall be magnified as you sit here laughing and grinning and trying to ignore the truth. And you'll never, ever shift that sense of guilt that resides in your hearts. Not for so long as you hide here."

"Father Loveford," Hendricks says as he

gets to his feet, "perhaps -"

"Save it," I reply, turning and heading back to the door. "Shame on you. Shame on all of you!"

Several voices call after me, but I ignore them. In my anger, I simply let the door swing shut and then make my way along the darkening evening street. In truth, I know I should have stayed and listened to what those men had to say, but I left because I was worried. I fear that, had I remained, I might have said something that I would ever-after regret.

I am starting to fear that the people of this village are beyond salvation.

***

Voices cry out in the distance, carrying far and wide through the forest as the last of the light fades. Bolton's men are still out there, still trying to track down the occupant of that tent. They shall not rest, I suppose, until they are satisfied that there is no spy.

I intended to go straight back to the church, but for some reason I ended up coming here to the edge of the forest instead. I would dearly like to go for a longer walk, to lose myself in nature for a while and to perhaps let my anger begin to subside, but I suppose there is a danger that Bolton's men might mistake me for a spy and shoot me on the spot. Such, it seems, is the state of the world today.

Yet as I stand here now, watching the distant flashlights of the airbase men, and as a cold wind blows against me and as night falls, I feel that I am at my lowest ebb. Bishop Carmichael told me to keep working, to remember the bigger picture, but I fear that I did not adequately convey to him the disastrous start that I have endured. How can I possibly get through to the people of Briarwych, when they won't even come to the church? Especially after I shouted at them all in the public house.

"Come out with your hands in the air!" one of the soldiers shouts far off in the forest. "We know you're here!"

I pause, before taking a step back. As much as I should like to go for a walk, I do not want to get drawn into the soldiers' madness, so I turn and start making my way back toward the church. I must admit that I feel utterly disconsolate, but I quickly remind myself that I am here as much for the airbase as for the village itself. If my lot is to sit out the next few years here, then so be it. I shall just have to make the best of a bad situation.

Once I reach the church, I push the door open and step inside. With the light outside fading, the church's interior is rather gloomy, but I suppose there is no point setting candles so late in the evening. I make my way along the corridor, heading toward the office, and then – at the last moment – I freeze as I realize what I just saw.

Out of the corner of my eye, I am certain that I spotted figures sitting facing the altar.

I hesitate for a few seconds, telling myself that I must have been wrong, but then I step back and look through the archway. To my surprise, I see that not only was I right, but I failed to see just how *many* figures are here.

The church is packed.

Every pew is taken, and some people are even standing at the sides. A few of the figures start turning to look this way, as if they only just heard me, and it is at that point that I realize I recognize several of these people from the public house, and from the streets of Briarwych.

I have a congregation.

"Please, Father," a woman says, with tears in her eyes, "we heard what you said in the pub tonight. You're right, we've been hiding from the truth. Please, you have to help us."

I stare at her, before looking out once more across the sea of heads. There must be over a hundred people here, huddled in the low light, and finally I start making my way along the aisle. I still cannot believe what I am seeing, yet – as I reach the front and turn to look properly – I see row after row of fearful faces staring back at me.

"You're right, Father," Hendricks says, from his seat on the front row. "We should all have come sooner, but we were scared. We don't know how to put this right."

"*Can* we put it right?" a woman asks, sitting a little further back. "Judith Prendergast was nobody's favorite round these parts, but we shouldn't have just left her here to rot. Someone should have come to check on her."

"Tell us how to be forgiven," another woman says, her voice trembling with sorrow. "Father, help us. We've all sinned."

"Sometimes," a man says nearby, "I think I'm going crazy. I'm scared I'll end up in an psychiatric hospital."

I pause, trying to work out what I might say, but then I make my way up to the pulpit. My knees feel weak and my hands are trembling, but it seems as if my outburst earlier has actually made people reconsider their actions. And as I stop in the pulpit and look out across the rows of faces, I realize that these people – these scared, guilt-laden people – truly *need* my help.

So I help them.

CHAPTER THIRTY-TWO

"BUT WE CAN TALK more about that on Sunday," I continue, my throat feeling rather dry now after I've been speaking for almost an hour. "That is, if you'll all come back on Sunday."

An immediate murmur rises from the congregation, and it is clear that they will indeed all return in a few days' time.

"For now," I add, "I imagine that you're all sick of the sound of my voice. Please remember, however, as you leave, that the Lord's forgiveness is always just a prayer away. The fact that you're all here this evening shows that you are willing to address your sins."

"Everyone's here, Father," Hendricks says from the front row. "I don't think a single soul from the village is anywhere else right now."

"I hope the same is true on Sunday," I reply with a faint smile. "Now please, it's getting late and I don't want to keep you any longer tonight. Go home, and sleep well tonight safe in the knowledge that you have all begun to tread the path to redemption. Amen."

"Amen," they all reply.

Taking a deep breath, I make my way down from the pulpit, which is a little tricky since the light is now so low. The stained-glass windows rise high above us all, as members of the congregation begin to rise and head toward the door, but precious little light is reaching us inside.

"Thank you, Father," a woman says, hurrying over to me and clutching my hands, then squeezing them tight. Tears are streaming down her face. "I just pray that the Lord can forgive me. I knew I should have come and checked on Miss Prendergast, but I just... I thought she was okay. I thought she'd left."

"It's alright," I tell her. "The Lord hears you."

"I've had dreams about her," another woman says as she approaches. "I've had the most horrible nightmares."

"I had more than dreams," a third woman adds, and I turn to see that Mrs. Canton has come over to join us. "Father, you know full well that I thought I saw Miss Prendergast outside the cottage once. Is it possible that guilt could have caused me to hallucinate?"

"Guilt can do many things to us," I reply. "I have a feeling that you shall sleep better tonight."

Hearing voices in the distance, I turn and see that few if any members of the congregation have left yet. They seem to be talking near the door.

"I've taken to having a glass of my husband's whiskey before bed," one of the women says, and I turn to see her wiping her nose on a handkerchief. "Oh, I know it's silly, but it helps me sleep, and it keeps me from having the worst of those dreams."

"Perhaps you could try sleeping without the whiskey tonight," I suggest, "so that your mind might rest."

Looking past her, I spot Mrs. Neill sitting alone on one of the pews, sobbing gently.

"Excuse me," I say to the others, before slipping past them and heading over to join the good lady. "My dear Mrs. Neill," I continue, "I must ask how you are coping."

"It's more than a month now since we heard anything," she says, with tears in her eyes. "A month, Father. That must mean something's happened, mustn't it? First we lost Jack, and now there's no news of Anthony out there in France."

Lowering her head, she puts her hands over her face, and a moment later I hear her starting to sniff back tears.

"First we lost one son, now the other."

"You don't know that," I point out. "Perhaps we can pray for his safe return."

"I can't do that," she replies. "I told you before. I can't pray for Anthony to be saved, not if it simply condemns some other mother's son to die."

"I'm not sure that's how it works."

"I can't," she whimpers, as tears run down from beneath her hands and trickle down her wrist. "I can't, Father. I just can't."

We remain in silence for a moment, both sitting on the cold pew. After a few seconds, Mrs. Neill looks up at the altar, and I see that tears are streaming down her face. In such times, I feel compelled to offer guidance and comfort, yet I know not what to say. This poor woman is suffering so terribly, and in these dark times she is far from alone. I still feel that I must help her, and finally I realize that there is one option that might work.

"Let us pray," I tell her.

"For Jack?"

"No, for -"

"I told you, I can't do that."

"Not for Anthony either," I continue, interrupting her. "Or rather, not solely for Anthony." I put my hands together. "Let us pray for all the sons out there in the theater of war."

"But if -"

"Whatever their nationality," I add.

She opens her mouth to argue with me, but then she hesitates. Perhaps, finally, I have managed to get through to her and make her see reason.

"Let us pray," I continue, "that for the sake of all young men, whether they're English or German or American or whatever, this dreadful fighting ends soon. For *all* of them, Mrs. Neill, across Europe and indeed across the world. Leaving not one of them out of our thoughts."

"Do you think that might work?" she asks.

"I think the Lord will listen," I tell her, "and that we can ask for no more than that."

"Why would he listen to *us*?" she asks. "Surely, so many others are already praying for peace? What does it matter if our voices are added?"

"We must have faith that our prayers will be heard. That our prayers shall join the prayers of mothers and fathers and sons and daughters all across the world, rising up from these war-torn lands and somehow joining together to be heard that much more clearly. Please, won't you join me?"

She stares at me for a moment, and then slowly she turns and bows her head. Clasping her hands together, she is clearly ready for prayer, which means that I must now rise to the occasion.

Turning, I bow my head and put my hands together, and then I close my eyes.

And the words come.

"We pray for an end to this madness," I say, as if the words are flowing through me from some other source, "and for the suffering, Lord, of your children to end. And let -"

Before I can finish, I realize that I can hear slightly raised voices coming from over by the doorway, and a moment later there's a faint banging sound.

"Excuse me, Mrs. Neill," I say, getting to my feet and then heading along the aisle.

As I reach the corridor, I see that a dozen or so men and women have gathered around the closed door, where they seem to be taking it in turns trying to get the door open.

"I think it's locked, Father," a woman says as I reach them.

"No, it's not locked," I reply, heading over to the door. "Perhaps it's a little stiff. Let me try."

I turn the handle, but then when I try to pull the door open I find that something is holding it firmly in place. I try several more times, and now it is apparent that there seems to be something on the other side that is keeping the door securely fastened.

"I know you're keen to have us here, Father," a man says, "but locking us inside seems a little extreme."

"The door is *not* locked," I reply, as I turn the handle again and again. "I do not understand."

"There isn't another way out, is there?" a

woman mutters. "What seems to be the problem, Father?"

"I do not understand," I tell her, as I turn the handle over and over without making any kind of breakthrough. "This is most unusual, it's almost as if -"

Suddenly I freeze, as I realize that I can hear a voice on the other side of the door. I lean closer and listen, but the voice seems muffled and quiet, as if somebody is speaking softly under their breath. I wait for a moment, trying to work out who I am hearing, and then I bang gently on the door.

"Excuse me," I call out, "but is somebody out there?"

"Who is it?" a man asks behind me.

I wait, but the person on the other side of the door fails to answer. I can still hear the muttering, however, so I step to one side and peer out through the narrow glass window above the alms box.

At first I see nobody, since the light is so low, but finally I crane my neck enough to make out a figure pacing back and forth in the gloom beyond the door. I reach out to bang on the window and ask what's going on, but then the figure turns slightly and I am shocked to see a face that I recognize.

"Lizzy?" I whisper, before tapping on the window. "Lizzy, can you open the door? Lizzy, what's happening out there?"

She turns and looks at me, and I am

immediately startled by the frenzied expression in her eyes. She looks almost wild.

"What's going on, Father?" a man asks nearby. "Are you getting us out of here, or what?"

"Lizzy!" I tap on the window again. "I don't know what you're doing, but I need you to unblock the door!"

I wait, but she seems to be talking to herself. And then, a moment later, she turns and scurries out of view, disappearing around the side of the church.

"Lizzy!"

I try the handle several more times, before taking a step back.

"What's up, Father?" another man asks. "We're not locked in the place, are we?"

"Where did she go?" I whisper, peering out the window again and seeing that Lizzy is still not back. It's almost as if she wasn't there in the first place, but I know that I saw her and I also know that she seemed to be talking to herself.

Suddenly I hear the sound of glass breaking behind me. Turning, I see that everybody else is looking toward the altar.

"What is it?" I ask, trying to stay calm despite a growing sense of panic. "What -"

Before I can finish, I'm shocked to see a bundle of flames come tumbling through the broken window and crash down onto the edge of the altar. A moment later a second bundle comes through, then a third.

"Let me through!" I shout, pushing past the people who are blocking my way as I struggle to reach the aisle. "Get out of my way!"

As the gathered congregation begins to panic, I race along the aisle, just as another flaming package falls into the church. This package, however, stops burning as it hits the altar, and then it rolls off the side and hits the ground before coming to a rest just as I get to the end of the aisle.

Looking down, I see that the bundle is wrapped in a cloth that has military stencils on the side.

"Put it out!" a voice shouts, and a moment later a man runs past me and throws a blanket over the burning packages.

Suddenly one of the packages explodes, sending me crashing back against the side of the pews. I roll onto my side and cover my face with my arms, just as a second package explodes and send a fireball rushing high up toward the rafters.

"What are those things?" a woman shouts, as others starts screaming. "Are they bombs? Are we being bombed?"

"The airbase," I whisper, as the flames merely burst through the blanket that the man is still trying to place over the last package. "These must be the experimental fuel packages from the -"

The third package explodes, knocking the

other man back against the wall.

Now three of the four packages are burning fast and brights, and the flames have already reached the first row of pews. I have never seen a fire like this before, but it's clear that the fuel inside the packages has begun to devour the wooden pews and is spreading faster and further than should be possible.

"Get back!" I shout, stumbling to my feet and waving at the villages to retreat. "Everybody get to the door!"

"It won't open!" a man yells, and I can hear the sound of other men frantically trying to break out of the church. "We're going to burn!"

"We're not going to burn," I reply, limping along the aisle before stopping and looking back at the flames that are now rising high from the altar. At the same time, thick black smoke is starting to fill the church, and it's clear that soon the smoke will be overwhelming. "This doesn't make sense, why would anybody do this?"

Everyone is trying to break the door down, so I head through to the office and try to break the window. The iron bars are too firm, however, so I hurry to the kitchen and then to the storeroom in a desperate attempt to find some other way out. Finding that one of the windows in the storeroom is a little larger than the others, I grab a broom and use the handle to start smashing the glass out of the way.

The handle's end hits the bars several times, but finally I knock out enough glass to drop the broom and start using my hands in a desperate attempt to pull the metal away. Even if this works, I'm not sure that anyone will be able to fit through, but it's the only chance.

Suddenly a face appears on the other side of the window, staring straight in at me with wild eyes.

"Lizzy!" I gasp. "You have to open the door! We're all going to die in here!"

"They deserve everything that's coming to them," she replies in a blank, monotone voice that betrays no emotion whatsoever. "For what they did to Mother."

"Revenge is never the answer!" I tell her. "Please, Lizzy, I know you're a good person. What happened to your mother was dreadful, but there are over a hundred people in here! Lizzy, you -"

Before I can finish, she steps out of view.

"Lizzy!" I shout, desperately trying to get her to talk to me. "Come back!"

Racing out of the room, I hurry into the next room, just in time to see Lizzy's shadow pass across the window.

"Lizzy, wait!" I yell, rushing to the window and banging my fists against the glass, as the increasingly thick smoke causes me to break into a coughing fit. "Lizzy, this is sheer madness!"

On the other side of the glass, her shadow hesitates for a moment, and I see her face turn to me.

"Lizzy," I continue, as people start screaming in the corridor, "I know you're angry and I know that what happened to your mother was terrible, but these people came to the church today and confessed their guilt. You don't need to -"

Suddenly I break down into another coughing fit, and it takes several seconds before I can speak again. Just as I open my mouth, however, Lizzy once more steps out of view.

"Wait!"

I race out of the room and over toward the door. Lights from the flames is filling the entire church now, and I have to push my way past the huddled figures of people who are staying low to avoid the worst of the smoke. Reaching the window next to the main door, I look out just in time to see Lizzy turning to me again.

"No!" I shout, banging my fists against the glass. "This isn't the way!"

The heat is getting stronger against the back of my neck, and I can tell that the flames are spreading with great speed. After a moment my knees begin to buckle, and I have to grab the side of the window in order to hold myself up. Already, the smoke is making it harder to see Lizzy as she stands outside.

"The Germans!" I gasp. "Lizzy, the flames will guide them straight to the airbase! You're going to... This is about much more than... Lizzy, please..."

Suddenly my grip slips, and I slump down against the stone floor. I can hear people cry out all around me, as the roar of the inferno gets stronger and stronger, but when I try to take a gulp of air I feel thick, acrid smoke filling my mouth and rushing down into my lungs. All I can do is try to shield my face as I turn away and claw at the wooden door, and finally my eyes slip shut.

CHAPTER THIRTY-THREE

SUDDENLY THE DOOR CLICKS OPEN, and I slump out onto the cold stone step.

Gasping, I begin to get up, only for somebody to slam into me from behind and shove me outside. I turn to go back into the church, but people are rushing out now and it's impossible to fight back. I have no choice but to pull out of the way, as the members of the congregation spill out through the door and race across the cemetery.

"Run!" I shout, grabbing any stragglers and hauling them out of the way as the church continues. "You must run! Get out of there! You must all run!"

More and more people come stumbling out. A moment later I hear a tremendous roaring sound, and I turn just in time to see a War Office truck screeching to a halt outside the cemetery gate. Soldiers from the airbase are already clambering out, and I watch as they begin to connect a hose to the huge container at the rear of the vehicle.

"What the hell's going on here?" Bolton yells, hurrying this way with his men. "Loveford! What happened?"

I try to answer, but I succeed merely in breaking down into a coughing fit. As I do so, several men carry one end of the hose into the church, and then I see the hose snap tight as the fire-fighting effort begins.

"This might have blown our cover!" Bolton shouts. "Do you realize what this means, man? This might be all Jerry needs!"

***

"Everyone's accounted for," Hendricks says, still a little breathless as he comes to find me next to the cemetery wall. "It's a miracle, isn't it? People helped each other, and they all got out."

"Are you sure?" I ask, looking over and watching as the walking wounded begin to make their ways back into the village. "Everyone's alright?"

"It's the shock that's a danger now," he continues. "Whatever can have happened, Father? I still don't understand how the fire started, or why we were locked inside."

I open my mouth to reply, but for a moment I'm not sure what to say. I am loathe to mention Lizzy's name before I know the full story, and I certainly don't want to bring up the subject of the experimental petrol that seems to have been used to start the conflagration. Then, blessedly, I'm saved by the sound of approaching footsteps, and I turn to see Bolton coming this way.

"The fire's out," he says darkly, as his men emerge from the church and head toward their vehicle. "So far, there's no report of German aircraft in the area, which means we've hopefully caught a lucky break." He pauses for a moment. "I need to get to the bottom of this, Loveford. First thing in the morning, we're going to start a full investigation and we won't stop until I know who started that fire and why. Do you know anything at all about it?"

I hesitate, before shaking my head.

"The culprit will face treason charges," Bolton continues. "He or she will hang, I'll make sure of that."

"I'm not sure that -"

Before I can finish, I spot a figure hurrying across the cemetery in the distance, scurrying quickly into the dark, empty church. Even from that brief flash of the figure's profile, I recognize her.

"I'm not sure that I can help you," I continue finally, turning to Bolton, "but I'll do what I can. At first light, we shall begin to examine the evidence."

"I'm still not writing off the possibility that it was a spy," he says, turning to walk away. After a moment, he glances back at me. "By the way, we looked more closely at some of the items in the tent, and there's a strong possibility that the occupant was a woman. Not that it matters, much. A woman's neck fits a noose just as well as a man's."

With that, he walks over to join his men at the truck. I remain where I am, watching as they pack up, and finally the vehicle trundles away along the road. I take a deep breath, and then I look around to make sure that nobody else is nearby, and then I begin to make my way back across the cemetery toward the church. As I get closer to the door, however, I slow my pace as I realize that I have no idea what to expect when I find Lizzy. Yes, she unlocked the door when she realized that she was endangering the airbase, but when I saw her through the window I spotted the eyes of a madwoman.

Finally, reaching the door, I look at the darkness ahead. Already, I can smell lingering wisps of smoke, and I fancy that I can feel some residual heat in the air too. Nevertheless, I know that I must face Lizzy, so I step inside and wait again for my eyes to adjust to the darkness.

I see her immediately.

She's kneeling on the floor, about halfway

along the corridor, almost completely hidden by shadows. She has her side to me, and she seems to be sobbing, so I take a couple of cautious steps forward.

I wait, but she does not react at all to my arrival.

"Lizzy," I say finally, my voice sounding so harsh and damaged after all the smoke that I inhaled. "What are you doing here?"

She mumbles something in reply, but I don't quite manage to make out the words.

"Lizzy," I say again, stepping a little closer, "I need you to look at me. Can you do that?"

I wait.

She remains slumped on the floor, barely visible in the darkness.

"Can you even hear me?" I continue. "Lizzy, can you -"

Suddenly she turns and looks at me, her face filled with fear. And in that same moment, her entire body is pulled backward along the corridor until she disappears into the shadows. She lets out a faint cry – half a cry, really – before falling silent again.

I open my mouth to call out to her, but for a few seconds I am struck dumb. Then, realizing that something seems to be terribly wrong, I take a few steps forward until I can once again – just about – see her.

She is once again slumped on the floor, although this time she is sitting up just a little and she is close to the church's gray stone wall.

"Lizzy," I say cautiously, "I -"

"She made me do it!" she blurts out, her voice filled with anguish and pain. "She made me, I didn't want to but she made me! She made me do it all!"

"What, Lizzy?" I ask. "What did she make you do?"

"I didn't want to," she sobs, as tears run from her eyes and mucus glistens beneath her nose. "You must believe me, Father Loveford! I didn't -"

Suddenly she turns her head slightly, as if she heard something in the darkness.

"I didn't!" she whimpers. "Stop saying that!"

"Lizzy, you're imagining things," I tell her. "You're not -"

"I didn't want to do it!" she yells, and suddenly she leans forward and bangs her head against the wall.

"Lizzy!" I shout. "Stop!"

"I didn't want to do any of it!" she screams, turning to me. There's now a cut on her forehead, just above her left eye, and it's clear now where her earlier bruises must have come from. "She made me, Father Loveford," she sobs. "She made me do all those wicked, wicked things!"

"Are you talking about your mother, Lizzy?"

I ask. "You must have loved her very much. I can tell that, but your mother... I am sorry, but your mother is dead, and you cannot take it upon yourself to punish those you deem responsible. Only God can stand in judgment upon their souls, and you must trust that he will see their true natures when the time comes."

I wait, but she's simply staring at me now. There are still tears on her cheeks, and her bottom lip is trembling.

"You mustn't listen to the voice," I continue, taking another step forward. "The voice is in your head."

Again I wait, and again she says nothing.

This time, however, I realize after a moment that I can hear a faint scratching sound, like fabric being torn or perhaps more like stone grinding against stone.

Lizzy shudders.

"Come to me," I say, as I reach my hand out toward her. "Lizzy, ignore the voice in your head and come to me."

She mumbles something, but once again I can't make out any of the words.

The scratching sound continues and, if anything, seems to be getting a little louder.

"It's over now," I say, stepping closer to Lizzy. "I shall get you the help that you need. Do you understand?"

She twitches, and then she leans forward slightly, out of the shadows.

"I'll help you," I continue, "and -"

Suddenly I stop, as I realize that I can see something moving in the shadows directly behind Lizzy. I open my mouth to ask what's happening, but then I squint slightly as I start to make out a shape.

Two hands.

Two pale, thin hands are reaching out from the darkness and digging their fingertips against Lizzy's back, grinding so hard and so deep that they're cutting through not only the fabric of her dress but also through the skin.

And on each hand, five sharp nails scratch against Lizzy's bones.

"What is that?" I whisper, as I feel my chest tighten with fear.

"I'm so sorry," Lizzy sobs, leaning a little further forward. "She made me do it. She made me do all of it."

The hands reach further out of the darkness, to keep scratching her, and in the process I see a face start to lean into the light. In an instant, I see that the face is thin and pale.

"She made me kill the poor man at the airbase," Lizzy whimpers, as the ghost of her mother grimaces and digs her fingertips harder against the bone, "to silence him. She made me steal the petrol. She told me to wait, she said eventually everyone would come to church, and that then I'd be able to avenge her death, but..."

She winces, as if she's in the most terrible pain.

"But I failed her," she continues finally, turning to me. "I was weak, I let them go. Don't you see now?"

"Lizzy, come to me," I say firmly, determined to get her away from this specter. I tell myself that this cannot be Judith Prendergast, for the woman is dead, yet I cannot deny what is right in front of me. "Lizzy, hurry. Lizzy! Now!"

I keep my head outstretched, but Lizzy merely twists around slightly as the scratching sound continues.

Staring at Judith Prendergast's face, I see that her features are contorted into an expression of pure hatred as she watches the back of her daughter's head. Indeed, as her grimace becomes even tighter, the scratching sound becomes more pronounced.

"Lizzy, get away from her immediately!" I shout, filled with panic as I rush forward and grab the poor girl's arm. At the same time, the air seems to turn bitter cold. "Lizzy! Now!"

"I'm sorry," she sobs, turning to me. "Father Loveford, I'm so, *so* sorry."

"If you -"

Before I can finish, Judith Prendergast turns and stares straight at me. I am briefly taken aback by the hellish sight of her dead black eyes, and then suddenly she lunges at me, screaming like a creature risen up from the depths of Hell.

CHAPTER THIRTY-FOUR

"LIZZY!"

Startled, I sit up and find that I am in the dark corridor. The air all around me is cold, but not as cold as before. Dazed for a moment, I cannot quite remember what happened, but then the memories come flooding back and I recall the sight of that terrible face rushing at me, and then...

And then what?

I fell back, and I think I must have knocked my head. I have no idea how long I was out, but I must have fallen unconscious, at least briefly. The night outside is still dark, so not too much time can have passed. As I stumble to my feet, however, I feel a pulsing pain in the back of my head, and I reach around to find that there seems to be a bruise. I must indeed have knocked myself out, but when I turn and look over my shoulder I see that the church's door is shut.

Did I close that when I came inside, or did somebody else?

I hesitate, before seeing that the door leading up to the bell-tower is open. That, I am sure, was shut earlier, and when I head over and look up the stairs I immediately hear a timid, terrified, sobbing voice coming from up in the tower itself.

"Lizzy?" I call out, before starting to hurry up. "Lizzy, wait! I'm coming!"

I slip several times, but finally I get to the upper floor and then I start scrambling up the narrowing staircase that leads to the very top of the tower. The sound of the distant voice is momentarily replaced by the sound of my own breathless gasps, but finally I fall out into the tower and see the terrible sight of Lizzy standing in one of the archways, silhouetted against the starry night sky as if she intends to leap from the tower.

I look around, but there is no sign of Judith Prendergast.

"Lizzy," I stammer, turning back to her. "It's me. I need you to come away from the edge."

I wait, but she does not reply.

"Lizzy!" I say more firmly, as I look around once again for any sign of that terrible, dead face. "Lizzy, we can work out later what has happened, but right now I need you to get down from there. Do you understand? It's dangerous."

Still not seeing any sign of Judith Prendergast, I edge across the tower until I am just a few feet behind Lizzy. I want to reach out and grab her, but as I look at the back of her head I cannot help but fear that she might take my movement as her cue to jump.

"Let me help you," I continue, as I start to very slowly reach out for her wrist. "Lizzy, things might seem bad now, but there's a way out of this. For a start, you needn't worry about what happened at the airbase. You have my solemn vow that I shall breathe not one word about any of this to Corporal Bolton. He'll never find out that you were responsible. Maybe that's wrong of me, but I won't let them get their hands on you. I just can't. They'd..."

They'd kill her.

I shan't say that to her, but it's true.

They'd try her for treason and they'd hang her.

"Come down with me," I tell her, as my hand edges closer to her wrist. I'm just inches away now, yet I fear what she might do when she feels my touch. I must move firmly and decisively.

I start counting down from three.

Two.

Suddenly hearing movement over my shoulder, I turn and see Judith Prendergast standing just a a few feet away. Instantly, my blood turns cold.

"You're not real," I whisper, trying desperately to convince myself. "You can't be real."

Her black eyes are fixed on Lizzy, and after a moment she takes a step toward us.

"You're not real!" I shout, although I can hear the tremor in my own voice. "In the name of all that's holy, I know that you cannot be real!"

She takes another step closer, and the air temperature dips noticeably around us.

"Stay back!" I snap. "You will not come anywhere near her, do you hear? You will not take so much as one more step!"

With her gaze still fixed on Lizzy's back, Judith Prendergast takes another step toward us.

"Lizzy, you must get down at once," I say, as I move into position to block the specter's advance. As I do so, I feel the chill air becoming colder still. "Lizzy, do you hear? Climb down from that ledge!"

Although I now have my back to her, I can tell that Lizzy has not done as she's told. I'd hear if she climbed down, but after a moment I feel the back of her dress fluttering in the breeze, brushing briefly against my shoulder. I want to turn and grab her, but I worry that by doing so I might cause her to fall. Besides, I know Lizzy and I am certain that she will not actually jump. To do so would mean certain death, and she would never waste her life in such a manner.

Judith Prendergast takes another step toward me, moving silently but keeping her black eyes fixed on Lizzy.

"Stop!" I say firmly. "In the name of the Lord, I command you to stop at once!"

She stops.

"The Lord compels you to stop!" I shout.

Judith Prendergast stares up at Lizzy for a moment longer, and then slowly – and silently – she turns and looks directly at me.

It is at this moment that I truly see her eyes are empty, for she possesses instead only two black pits that seem to speak of her soullessness.

"You are an abomination," I stammer, my voice trembling again with a fear that I cannot suppress. "You are ungodly. Leave this house of the Lord and do not come back. Your transgression here is over."

She stares at me for a few seconds, before tilting her head slightly.

"Flee, dark spirit," I continue, "for you..."

My voice trails off as I see a smile slowly starting to spread across her lips.

"You are an abomination," I say again, struggling to think of the right words. "You are not right here. By that I mean that you desecrate the very ground upon which you stand and..."

Her smile is growing.

It is as if my words cause her nothing but amusement.

"How dare you set foot in this church?" I ask, but now my voice is almost falling apart with weakness, no matter how hard I try to stay strong. "You are -"

Suddenly she looks back at Lizzy, and then slowly she raises her left hand and starts reaching past me.

"Stop!" I gasp, turning just as Judith's pale thin hand touches Lizzy's shoulder. "You cannot do this, you -"

Before I can finish, Judith places her other hand on Lizzy's back, just beneath the torn and bloodied fabric of her dress, and pushes.

Lifelessly, helplessly, Lizzy topples forward.

"No!" I shout, lunging through the archway and desperately trying to grab Lizzy. My right hand almost reaches her ankle, but falls short by a few inches.

My left hand then manages to grab her other ankle, but in the process I am pulled forward until I am almost all the way out of the bell-tower myself. Somehow I manage to grab hold of the edge and steady myself, but then I look down and see that I am barely managing to hold on to Lizzy as she dangles in the night air. For a moment, I can only stare in horror at the ground far, far below.

Gasping, I start pulling Lizzy up. I am not a strong man, but in this hour of need I somehow find a strength that I never knew I possessed. I struggle a little, but finally I manage to drag us both back into the bell-tower. Lizzy slumps down against the floor, and I turn and see in the moonlight that her eyes are still open.

"Lizzy!" I say firmly, touching the side of her face and finding that her skin is so very cold. "Say something! Lizzy, can you hear me?"

She does not reply, so I quickly check her pulse and find to my relief that she is indeed alive. Catatonic, but alive. Then I turn and look around, terrified in case I might spot Judith Prendergast again, but for now the spectral vision seems to have departed. I look around for a moment longer, still convinced that Judith might at any moment emerge from the shadows, but then I realize that the time for this sort of thing shall come later.

Grabbing hold of Lizzy, I mumble an apology for my forcefulness and then I begin to gather her into my arms. As I do so, however, I see something slip from her hand. A small, folded photograph lands on the floor, and when I pick it up I see that it shows the stern face of a woman.

It is the same woman I saw a moment ago, and when I turn the photograph over I see a handwritten scrawl on the reverse.

One word:

Mother.

This must be Judith Prendergast, and it is the first time that I have ever seen her face. In that case, how did I *see* the face before me when the specter first appeared?

Unless the specter is real.

I hesitate for a moment, before realizing that there will be time to come to an understanding later. Forcing myself to stay focused, I finish gathering Lizzy up into my arms, before getting to my feet and carrying her toward the stairs. All I know at this moment is that I have to get her out of here, that once we've escaped the church I shall be able to get her the care that she needs. I shall be able, too, to work out what exactly has happened here tonight. I still believe that the specter – while certainly very vivid and terrifying – cannot possibly be the spirit of Judith Prendergast, yet if that is the case how did I see her likeness before I saw the photograph?

Struggling to maneuver in the narrow stairwell, I nevertheless manage to get Lizzy down to the next floor, and then the next set of steps is rather easier. Lizzy remains motionless in my arms as I carry her down to the dark corridor, and I tell her that everything will be alright as I start hurrying to the door.

And then I stop, as I see Judith Prendergast standing in our way, watching us black-eyed from a patch of moonlight that lends her face an ethereal, almost glowing pale quality.

I stand completely still for a moment, with Lizzy still in my arms, as I realize that I have no choice. If I am to get Lizzy and myself out of the church, I must walk straight past the ghost of Judith Prendergast. She is blocking the way, and even from here I can see that same expression of hatred on her face.

My knees are trembling and might buckle at any moment, but I take a cautious step forward, then another, carrying Lizzy ever-closer to the ghoul.

"You're not real," I whisper, hoping to convince myself of that fact and – in the process – to make the frightful vision disappear. "I know you're not."

I get closer, and closer still, until I am barely more than half a dozen steps from the woman, with the door another couple of steps behind her, and then I stop. It is as if fear has seized my legs and now keeps me from going any further.

"You're not real," I stammer, barely managing to get the words out as I see that Judith Prendergast's hollow eyes remain fixed on Lizzy. "You're... I... you're..."

I pause for a moment.

And that's when I realize the truth.

"You *are* real," I whisper. "How would I have known your face before I saw that photograph? You are real and..."

My voice trails off.

For a few seconds, I can only marvel at the perverse beauty of this sight. The dead woman stands before me, looking every bit alive save for the miraculous hollows of her eyes. At the same time, the more I observe her, the more I realize that she seems to draw in the light from the air around her, blackening the room. There is something else, though, something about her that chills my soul, and it takes a moment before I finally realize what is wrong: she is not breathing. One does not usually notice other people's breaths, but as I stare at Judith Prendergast I see that her body is still within. There are no breaths, there is no beating heart.

There is only the hatred on her face, tightening into a sneer as she continues to look at her daughter.

And she is powerless.

"You can't hurt her," I say out loud, as I come to understand the limits of her powers. "Not now. If you could hurt her, you'd have done it by now. Maybe you can whisper in her ear and convince her to leap to her death, but you can't really *do* anything to her. Maybe you can scratch her back from time to time, but that's not enough for you, is it? Even that push in the bell-tower was more a hint than a proper push. Maybe the push was the absolute strongest move you could make and -"

Suddenly she snarls and leans closer to Lizzy.

"And that's all you can do!" I stammer, although at the same time I instinctively take a step back. "You can't even leave the church, can you? Otherwise you'd have wrought your revenge upon the villagers long ago. Mrs. Canton didn't actually see you from her window that night, it was just a guilt-induced vision. You're trapped here in the place of your death, and you'll be trapped here forever, which means I only have to get Lizzy away from you, which means..."

I look past her, toward the door, and in that instant I know what I must do.

She snarls again. A cruel, angry snarl, but also one that is utterly impotent.

"You *are* real," I tell her, "but that doesn't matter. Not once we're out of this place."

I pause for a moment, before taking a deep breath. Everything I think I know about the world is crumbling, but I know that I have no choice, even as I feel my sanity beginning to slip.

And then, finally, I look down at Lizzy as I take a step forward, followed by another step, then another. I feel a freezing cold shudder, and my knees are trembling with fear, but I step straight through Judith Prendergast's ghost and then I fumble for the door handle.

It takes a few seconds before I manage to

turn the handle, but I manage to get the door open and then I step out into the cold night air. I step forward again, then again, with Lizzy still in my arms, and then slowly I turn and look back at Judith Prendergast.

She is staring at me.

Suddenly she screams, unleashing a howl of rage and fury. She comes at me, but as she approaches the church's threshold she fades entirely from sight until she is gone.

Holding my breath, I wait in case she reappears.

A moment later, the door slams shut with such force that I hear the entire frame shudder.

Immediately, my knees buckle and I drop to the floor, inadvertently spilling Lizzy from my arms in the process. I manage to protect her head, keeping her from injury, and then I roll her over and look down at her poor, beautiful face.

"Lizzy!" I gasp, forcing her eyes open, only for them to slip shut again as soon as I let go.

I shake her shoulder, but she seems incapable of waking.

"Help!" I shout, looking toward the cemetery gate, hoping that somebody out there will hear me as I continue to shake her prone body. "Help us!"

I look around, but there is still no sign of anybody coming to our assistance. Have these people all run away?

And then, as I am about to call out again, I happen to look toward the church. It is in that moment that my heart chills, and that I see a figure watching us from the other side of one of the windows. The glass is mottled and dirty, but I can just about make out a deathly pale face still staring straight at us from inside the church. Still watching. Still filled with pure, unadulterated, never-ending hatred.

EPILOGUE

One year later

"MAY THE LORD HEAR ME, and guide me through it all."

Keeping my head bowed, so as not to be noticed, I make my way along the corridor. Voices are shouting out in the distance, patients and nurses, as I head toward the exit. I can see the double-doors up ahead, and the glorious sunshine beyond, and now I am only a few meters away. If I just keep walking, and don't look back, I shall be fine.

"Father?"

Suddenly a hand touches my shoulder from behind, and I freeze.

"Father Loveford, where are you going?"

I half turn to look at her, but I already know

that this is Nurse Simpkins.

"Father, why don't you come back this way with me?"

"I -"

"Please, Father. You know it's important."

I hesitate, before turning fully and seeing her kind face smiling back at me.

"I know you weren't really going to leave," she continues, "were you?"

After staring at her for a moment, I turn and look once again along the corridor. The daylight seems so bright outside, and I can see the beautiful green gardens stretching out toward a distant treeline. And then, looking up at the panel above the door, I feel my heart sink as I see – etched in reverse in the glass – the name of this place:

Meadow's Downe Asylum

"Come on, Father," Nurse Simpkins says, moving her hand down to my elbow. "You don't need me to tell you, do you? You know you have to come with me."

"I wasn't leaving," I reply, although I can hear my voice trembling. "I was just going to fetch something from my bicycle."

"You were?"

She pauses, before letting go of my elbow.

"I'm sorry, Father," she continues, sounding

a little relieved. "Please forgive me. It's just that... You mustn't be discouraged, that's all. She'll recognize you soon, I'm sure of it. You must just give her more time." There are tears in her eyes now. "Please, Father Loveford, don't give up on her."

"I would never," I reply. "I *could* never. I'm just going to the bicycle, and then I'll be back. I promise."

***

Stopping at the bicycle, I open the basket at the front and take out the small bunch of flowers that I brought today. The flowers were purchased at the local market in Fetchford, and they're yellow and purple. Just the colors that Lizzy always said she likes.

***

"At least he gave me his word on that score," I say as I finish arranging the flowers in a vase on the windowsill. "Bishop Carmichael has issued an irrevocable decree. Briarwych Church shall remain locked forever. Nobody will ever so much as unlock that door again. Just in case..."

I pause for a moment, thinking back to the horrific sight of Judith Prendergast's dead face, and then I turn and look over at the bed.

Lizzy is still flat on her back, still staring up at the ceiling the same way she has been staring for the past twelve months. Occasionally she blinks, at night she sleeps, but otherwise she shows no sign that she is aware of the world around her. It is as if her experience at Briarwych, and the haunting sight of her dead mother's spirit, left her mind completely ruined and incapable of returning to normal.

Still, Doctor Ferguson and Doctor Stewart both say that there is hope.

Patients have woken from longer, deeper reveries in the past, I am told. Lizzy responds to certain basic forms of external stimulation, for example to pain when a needle is pushed against one of her fingertips, and I am told that this is a very good sign. I am advised to keep talking to her, to keep chatting away, which is one of the reasons why I come here every single day – even Sundays – and waffle on about inconsequential matters so that she might hear my voice.

One day, she will wake up.

Yes, I'm sure of that.

And when it happens, I intend to be here to welcome her back to the world.

"You're safe now," I tell her as I take a seat next to her bed. "It's been a year now and there's been no sign of your mother. I can't profess to understand how or why, but it seems that her spirit cannot stray far from Briarwych Church. Not that I am even certain that what we saw that night was..."

My voice trails off as I think back to that awful moment in the bell-tower, to the moment when Judith Prendergast screamed and lunged at Lizzy. As much as I do not want to believe that such things are possible, I know deep down that what I saw that night was real. I cannot explain how it happened, but it seems that for some reason Judith Prendergast was indeed able to return after her death and drive her daughter to commit terrible acts and, ultimately, to madness.

But now she is gone. Or, at least, far from here.

"The weather is rather good today," I tell Lizzy, hoping that perhaps I might interest her in the world once more. "A little warmer than of late, and the wind has not been so biting. Indeed, on my way here I noticed some fresh patches of bluebells by the side of the road, and that is often indicative of a change in the season. You would like the view from the hill, I am sure. Perhaps some time we shall be able to take a short walk out there."

I watch Lizzy's face for a moment, but there is no hint of recognition. It is as if – as usual – she has not even noticed my arrival.

"Yes, a walk would be very nice," I add, as I turn and look out the window. "Perhaps later in the year, before autumn. Then again, the autumnal tones can be quite beautiful, so there is no need to hurry. It might even be better to wait. Have I told you about the view from the hill? Oh, it's utterly magnificent. You'll love it, Lizzy. Truly, you'll feel a sense of peace there that's unlike any you've ever felt before."

As I continue to talk to Lizzy, I feel a growing sense of calm. She'll wake up soon, I know she will. She must. And she will make the most wonderful wife, just as soon as she is released from this asylum.

THE HAUNTING OF BRIARWYCH CHURCH

Also by Amy Cross

The Devil, the Witch and the Whore
(The Deal book 1)

"Leave the forest alone. Whatever's out there, just let it be. Don't make it angry."

When a horrific discovery is made at the edge of town, Sheriff James Kopperud realizes the answers he seeks might be waiting beyond in the vast forest. But everybody in the town of Deal knows that there's something out there in the forest, something that should never be disturbed. A deal was made long ago, a deal that was supposed to keep the town safe. And if he insists on investigating the murder of a local girl, James is going to have to break that deal and head out into the wilderness.

Meanwhile, James has no idea that his estranged daughter Ramsey has returned to town. Ramsey is running from something, and she thinks she can find safety in the vast tunnel system that runs beneath the forest. Before long, however, Ramsey finds herself coming face to face with creatures that hide in the shadows. One of these creatures is known as the devil, and another is known as the witch. They're both waiting for the whore to arrive, but for very different reasons. And soon Ramsey is offered a terrible deal, one that could save or destroy the entire town, and maybe even the world.

Also by Amy Cross

The Soul Auction

"I saw a woman on the beach. I watched her face a demon."

Thirty years after her mother's death, Alice Ashcroft is drawn back to the coastal English town of Curridge. Somebody in Curridge has been reviewing Alice's novels online, and in those reviews there have been tantalizing hints at a hidden truth. A truth that seems to be linked to her dead mother.

"Thirty years ago, there was a soul auction."

Once she reaches Curridge, Alice finds strange things happening all around her. Something attacks her car. A figure watches her on the beach at night. And when she tries to find the person who has been reviewing her books, she makes a horrific discovery.

What really happened to Alice's mother thirty years ago? Who was she talking to, just moments before dropping dead on the beach? What caused a huge rockfall that nearly tore a nearby cliff-face in half? And what sinister presence is lurking in the grounds of the local church?

Also by Amy Cross

Darper Danver: The Complete First Series

Five years ago, three friends went to a remote cabin in the woods and tried to contact the spirit of a long-dead soldier. They thought they could control whatever happened next. They were wrong...

Newly released from prison, Cassie Briggs returns to Fort Powell, determined to get her life back on track. Soon, however, she begins to suspect that an ancient evil still lurks in the nearby cabin. Was the mysterious Darper Danver really destroyed all those years ago, or does her spirit still linger, waiting for a chance to return?

As Cassie and her ex-boyfriend Fisher are finally forced to face the truth about what happened in the cabin, they realize that Darper isn't ready to let go of their lives just yet. Meanwhile, a vengeful woman plots revenge for her brother's murder, and a New York ghost writer arrives in town to uncover the truth. Before long, strange carvings begin to appear around town and blood starts to flow once again.

Also by Amy Cross

The Ghost of Molly Holt

"Molly Holt is dead. There's nothing to fear in this house."

When three teenagers set out to explore an abandoned house in the middle of a forest, they think they've found the location where the infamous Molly Holt video was filmed.

They've found much more than that...

Tim doesn't believe in ghosts, but he has a crush on a girl who does. That's why he ends up taking her out to the house, and it's also why he lets her take his only flashlight. But as they explore the house together, Tim and Becky start to realize that something else might be lurking in the shadows.

Something that, ten years ago, suffered unimaginable pain.

Something that won't rest until a terrible wrong has been put right.

Also by Amy Cross

American Coven

He kidnapped three women and held them in his basement. He thought they couldn't fight back. He was wrong...

Snatched from the street near her home, Holly Carter is taken to a rural house and thrown down into a stone basement. She meets two other women who have also been kidnapped, and soon Holly learns about the horrific rituals that take place in the house. Eventually, she's called upstairs to take her place in the ice bath.

As her nightmare continues, however, Holly learns about a mysterious power that exists in the basement, and which the three women might be able to harness. When they finally manage to get through the metal door, however, the women have no idea that their fight for freedom is going to stretch out for more than a decade, or that it will culminate in a final, devastating demonstration of their new-found powers.

Also by Amy Cross

The Ash House

Why would anyone ever return to a haunted house?

For Diane Mercer the answer is simple. She's dying of cancer, and she wants to know once and for all whether ghosts are real.

Heading home with her young son, Diane is determined to find out whether the stories are real. After all, everyone else claimed to see and hear strange things in the house over the years. Everyone except Diane had some kind of experience in the house, or in the little ash house in the yard.

As Diane explores the house where she grew up, however, her son is exploring the yard and the forest. And while his mother might be struggling to come to terms with her own impending death, Daniel Mercer is puzzled by fleeting appearances of a strange little girl who seems drawn to the ash house, and by strange, rasping coughs that he keeps hearing at night.

The Ash House is a horror novel about a woman who desperately wants to know what will happen to her when she dies, and about a boy who uncovers the shocking truth about a young girl's murder.

Also by Amy Cross

Haunted

Twenty years ago, the ghost of a dead little girl drove Sheriff Michael Blaine to his death.

Now, that same ghost is coming for his daughter.

Returning to the small town where she grew up, Alex Roberts is determined to live a normal, quiet life. For the residents of Railham, however, she's an unwelcome reminder of the town's darkest hour.

Twenty years ago, nine-year-old Mo Garvey was found brutally murdered in a nearby forest. Everyone thinks that Alex's father was responsible, but if the killer was brought to justice, why is the ghost of Mo Garvey still after revenge?

And how far will the real killer go to protect his secret, when Alex starts getting closer to the truth?

Haunted is a horror novel about a woman who has to face her past, about a town that would rather forget, and about a little girl who refuses to let death stand in her way.

Also by Amy Cross

The Curse of Wetherley House

"If you walk through that door, Evil Mary will get you."

When she agrees to visit a supposedly haunted house with an old friend, Rosie assumes she'll encounter nothing more scary than a few creaks and bumps in the night. Even the legend of Evil Mary doesn't put her off. After all, she knows ghosts aren't real. But when Mary makes her first appearance, Rosie realizes she might already be trapped.

For more than a century, Wetherley House has been cursed. A horrific encounter on a remote road in the late 1800's has already caused a chain of misery and pain for all those who live at the house. Wetherley House was abandoned long ago, after a terrible discovery in the basement, something has remained undetected within its room. And even the local children know that Evil Mary waits in the house for anyone foolish enough to walk through the front door.

Before long, Rosie realizes that her entire life has been defined by the spirit of a woman who died in agony. Can she become the first person to escape Evil Mary, or will she fall victim to the same fate as the house's other occupants?

Also by Amy Cross

The Ghosts of Hexley Airport

Ten years ago, more than two hundred people died in a horrific plane crash at Hexley Airport.

Today, some say their ghosts still haunt the terminal building.

When she starts her new job at the airport, working a night shift as part of the security team, Casey assumes the stories about the place can't be true. Even when she has a strange encounter in a deserted part of the departure hall, she's certain that ghosts aren't real.

Soon, however, she's forced to face the truth. Not only is there something haunting the airport's buildings and tarmac, but a sinister force is working behind the scenes to replicate the circumstances of the original accident. And as a snowstorm moves in, Hexley Airport looks set to witness yet another disaster.

Also by Amy Cross

The Girl Who Never Came Back

Twenty years ago, Charlotte Abernathy vanished while playing near her family's house. Despite a frantic search, no trace of her was found until a year later, when the little girl turned up on the doorstep with no memory of where she'd been.

Today, Charlotte has put her mysterious ordeal behind her, even though she's never learned where she was during that missing year. However, when her eight-year-old niece vanishes in similar circumstances, a fully-grown Charlotte is forced to make a fresh attempt to uncover the truth.

Originally published in 2013, the fully revised and updated version of *The Girl Who Never Came Back* tells the harrowing story of a woman who thought she could forget her past, and of a little girl caught in the tangled web of a dark family secret.

Also by Amy Cross

Asylum
(The Asylum Trilogy book 1)

"No-one ever leaves Lakehurst. The staff, the patients, the ghosts... Once you're here, you're stuck forever."

After shooting her little brother dead, Annie Radford is sent to Lakehurst psychiatric hospital for assessment. Hearing voices in her head, Annie is forced to undergo experimental new treatments devised by a mysterious old man who lives in the hospital's attic. It soon becomes clear that the hospital's staff, led by the vicious Nurse Winter, are hiding something horrific at Lakehurst.

As Annie struggles to survive the hospital, she learns more about Nurse Winter's own story. Once a promising young medical student, Kirsten Winter also heard voices in her head. Voices that traveled a long way to reach her. Voices that have a plan of their own. Voices that will stop at nothing to get what they want.

What kind of signals are being transmitted from the basement of the hospital? Who is the old man in the attic? Why are living human brains kept in jars? And what is the dark secret that lurks at the heart of the hospital?

Also by Amy Cross

The Devil's Hand

"I felt it last night! I was all alone, and suddenly a hand touched my shoulder!"

The year is 1943. Beacon's Ash is a private, remote school in the North of England, and all its pupils are fallen girls. Pregnant and unmarried, they have been sent away by their families. For Ivy Jones, a young girl who arrived at the school several months earlier, Beacon's Ash is a nightmare, and her fears are strengthened when one of her classmates is killed in mysterious circumstances.

Has the ghost of Abigail Cartwright returned to the school? Who or what is responsible for the hand that touches the girls' shoulders in the dead of night? And is the school's headmaster Jeremiah Kane just a madman who seeks to cause misery, or is he in fact on the trail of the Devil himself? Soon ghosts are stalking the dark corridors, and Ivy realizes she has to face the evil that lurks in the school's shadows.

The Devil's Hand is a horror novel about a girl who seeks the truth about her friend's death, and about a madman who believes the Devil stalks the school's corridors in the run-up to Christmas.

For more information, visit:

www. amycross.com

AMY CROSS

Printed in Great Britain
by Amazon